The
Mark Widdowson
BLOGS

Adrian G R Scott

authorHOUSE®

AuthorHouse™
1663 Liberty Drive
Bloomington, IN 47403
www.authorhouse.com
Phone: 1-800-839-8640

Published by AuthorHouse   02/01/2013

ISBN: 978-1-4817-8101-5 (sc)
ISBN: 978-1-4817-8100-8 (e)

If you are unfamiliar with the locations mentioned in these pages go to Wikipedia and Google to give you a bit of background, especially look up Edlington. Look at Google Maps for a sense of the geography of South Yorkshire and check out any websites that give statistics about social and economic deprivation. Look up the Peak District for an appreciation of why Jess was so drawn to this area for silence and solace.

Sheffield
June
2012

Why I am Publishing This

My name is Mark Widdowson, I am a twenty-eight year old journalist, maybe not a brilliant reporter but one who managed to get a story any hack in the business would kill for.

I left school at sixteen with a couple of GCSE's one of them in English. I bummed around for a number of years working in pubs and then as a waiter. Then I realised that what I loved was writing stories and I rode the internet wave with a blog about the Sheffield music scene which attracted a few hundred followers.

I met a journalist from the Doncaster Free Press at a gig one night and she got me thinking about submitting pieces for the paper. Amazingly they liked them and I got work as a Freelance, covering gigs and then gradually they sent me to other jobs as they came to trust my copy. As I lived in Sheffield I offered some pieces to the Sheffield Star and Telegraph and I almost made a living, though a pretty precarious one.

Last year I was sent to cover a developing story about Jess Jennings this forty-year-old hairdresser from Edlington. I was told there had been a commotion at St Peter in Chains, Doncaster's Catholic Church, this homeless guy had been causing trouble and the Jennings woman prevented the parishioners from calling the Police and was reputed to have sparked a massive change in the man. Rumours spread that she was a healer and was causing quite a stir. So my Editor, who was always on the lookout for the strange and peculiar to spice up the paper, was on it in a flash. I was sent because I had shown a bit of a flair for Church stories.

You see my other GCSE was in RE and being Roman Catholic, growing up going to Church I understood how it all worked. I had covered a few fetes and a story about a vicar having a couple of affairs in a Doncaster Parish which ultimately made it into the tabloids, always a feather in the cap if your story goes national.

I interviewed the down and out guy and Jess had obviously affected him deeply. I stopped going to mass as soon as I was old enough to decide for myself and rarely thought about religion, unless it was part of a story but I do have to admit to becoming obsessed with Jess Jennings. She was not like anyone I had ever met. Things always happened around her; there was never a dull moment. At first my interest was because she made such good copy but it didn't take long for it to become personal. I tried on a number of occasions to get an interview with her and she, as she always did with the press, refused point blank.

Then when I was out in Bamford on the day she met the lad who had escaped from a psychiatric ward, I was going to file the story with the Star, but she grabbed me on the train back to Sheffield and said that if I was ready to stop working for the Press she would give me exclusive interviews and access to her work. What a choice, where do I publish then, I asked her, write an independent blog, she said. She told me that she wanted people to know about her work for the Great Turning from the point of view of someone like me, someone who has all the instincts and independence of a journalist, but without an Editor's axe grinding in the background.

So that's what you have in your hands now, my blogs, written quickly from the frontline of Jess Jennings's extraordinary journey. I wrote them as they happened, on the hoof. Just posted them up there and then went off again chasing after her, all over the country. The Editors I had worked for were going crazy for more copy as she became more and more notorious. I could have made a fortune.

But what had been a journalist's fascination became a personal odyssey. I never dreamed that I was caught up in such a remarkable chain of events. The days in London were astonishing and what happened to her at the hands of the authorities demands to be told. I want it out there before they catch up with me and try to silence me. So I have just tidied up the blogs using what I know now, they are, however, from my vantage point, the unvarnished truth.

I have tried not to put too much of my own spin on what happened so that you can make up your own mind about her. I have to tell you that I would be very dubious about her if I read these blogs for the first time, but I want to guarantee that this is what I saw and heard, in fact some of it is from the horse's mouth! I don't know what I make of the last part, she did not reappear to me personally but I spoke with others close to her who say they saw her and I do trust them, they have no reason to bullshit me.

When this comes out I will be abroad, I am scared of the consequences and need to be somewhere they cannot reach me. My blog was taken down a few times and I had to keep reposting it on new sites. In the end I gave up and have used the money given to me by one of her Agents for Change to self publish this book. However you have got hold of it, think that maybe you were meant to read it.

Make of it what you will, but ask yourself this question, whatever you think happened to Jess Jennings after her death, what would make the powers that be in this country and beyond feel so threatened that they decided to do away with her?

Beginnings This is how it all started, and I was there from very early on. It is an account of Jess Jennings, a woman who seemed, by the end of the affair like the personification of an astonishing energy or verve; religious people would call her a Guru or a Prophet, (though many of them seemed to despise her), political types saw her as a leader, even a revolutionary (though the authorities quickly saw her as a threat, even an insurgent). Many who met her said she gave them a deep sense of the meaning of life and made that meaning achievable. None of this, however was obvious at first glance, she was ordinary. When I think about Jess in the early days it seems outrageous to make any of these claims.

First Blog
Edlington
May 2011

A Messenger Back then there was one character that had all the unconventional types looking

4

for someone or something. Some people said that he was predicted in the Mayan prophecies and the New Age Websites were full of such prognostications. They all seemed to agree that a messenger was coming and that he would usher in a new era or as some said, (like they always do), the end of the world. One person I interviewed said that hosts of people had all had the same dream where a voice was shouting in a desert:

'*Look a broadcaster is coming and he will sound the alert!*'

These websites and the people I met all agreed on the message,

'*Get ready for something new, get your heads straight, get ready for a change*'.

That was backed up by my own encounter with the man, when I finally saw and heard him for myself; he was like a powerful voice sounding in the urban deserts and in the deserted wild places.

Jed called Rumi

He was called Jed but he had changed his name to Jalaladin Rumi[1] (when he had become a Sufi Muslim), springing up from nowhere, he wore long maroon robes and he didn't drink alcohol or eat meat. He would recite mystical poetry and speak directly to the heart of things. He didn't go with women or men. He was a nature type, one of those survival geeks. He knew what to eat in the wild, berries and fruit and where to find roots full of carbohydrate. People seemed to sense the places he would appear and would go there in droves. Some of these places were deserted building sites but his favourite spot was out in the brooks around Grindleford, in the Peak District.

He would stand waist deep in the water, people would come down and he would make them strip naked and then lay them back into the river, totally immerse them and hold them there for a good minute or so. When they came up he

---

[1]   After the Great Persian Poet

would give them a red cotton scarf as sign of the change. They came to call him the *Drowner*.

The Drowning He told the people who came out to him, and believe me these weren't just hippy types, there were Estate Agents, Lawyers and Nurses, Students and Teachers, Street People and Sex Workers, and he said that this was a way of dying. He warned them not to do it unless they were prepared to let go of their addictions and dependencies, unless they were prepared to live a new life. This new life was like the life people lead when they know they have months to live, a life of nourishing priorities. This was nothing like the baptism done in Churches with drops of water on babies' heads; in fact he never mentioned baptism, he only ever called it *The Drowning*.

He went on to say *'I am not the real star of the show here. She is coming very soon, I am just the opening credits, but she is the whole movie. My drowning is just a beginning, a change for a few days maybe, hers will plunge you into a whole new world, then you won't be in the know, you will be in the mystery!'*

Jess from Edlington It was around this time that Jess came from Edlington, a former pit village outside Rotherham, coming on the train to Grindleford and up the valley to find Rumi. He plunged her into the brook, right under the water, for more than two minutes and then up she came gasping and breathless. Then a shaft of sunlight shone straight onto her, she told me later that she felt a great and beautiful bird, (maybe an Owl), had flown down and somehow reached into her and she heard a voice saying

'You, right now, are the most loveable, the most ready to love, and your Great Emergence is here'

Visions on Kinder Immediately after this that same force dragged her stumbling up onto Kinder Scout, the most remote and desolate

6

place, known as the Dark Peak. For nearly a month and a half she lived up there, eating nothing, she must have drunk something or she would have died, but she had no tent, she just survived. During that time she saw all kinds of possibilities, hunger created hallucinations and visions but she just kept her feet on the ground and waited for the guidance that had come with the bird to grow inside her.

At first the place seemed to match the wildness and fears of her night terrors but gradually she realised they were no danger to her and that she had friends and companions, the animals of the wilderness. She even spoke of the revelations she experienced; that the darkest things both inner and outer became her helpers and that strange powers came and cared for her.

The Drowner Taken In time Rumi was finally arrested; the police said he was causing a public nuisance by drawing such great crowds out to a tourist area. It was rumoured that the Police planted Cocaine and Magic Mushrooms on his person to discredit him. They held him on remand until he could be charged, there was talk of him being some kind of agitator and that he had links with al-Qaeda.

Jess came down from Kinder Scout at this time and travelled by bus back to Doncaster and began speaking anywhere people would gather and listen, parish rooms, memorial halls, pubs and working men's clubs. She said that she had a message given to her by the Great Silence:

It's Time *'It's time, right now, to change, not just to think about it, but to do it. The change is there waiting inside for you to find it. A change that comes not from buying something or joining something, no those things won't make you happy. Happiness grows inside. Accept this now and you will never be the same again, this is the Great Emergence!'*

Going down Edlington High Street Jess caught sight of two men, Rob Stuart and Andy Green on their way to sign on;

they were in their mid twenties, they had been in and out of casual work all their adult lives as had their fathers, ever since the pit closed down.

Jess said to them, *'Lads, I know you are totally fed up with being on the dole, why don't you come with me and I will show you a different kind of work. A job that takes up all your time and energy and you will become agents of change.'*

They looked at each other, initially bemused to be spoken to in that way by a woman, yet she exuded such a powerful sense of purpose that they shrugged, and went straight after her; they did not even stop to sign on.

In the Tasty Bites café down the street, Jess saw a brother and sister, Joe and Julie Marsh, eating bacon sandwiches and looking at the jobs page in the Advertiser. Jess, Rob and Andy went in and sat down with them. She made the same invitation to Joe and Julie, again both in their mid twenties, and like the other two they put down the newspaper, finished their tea and went with her.

An Ex Hairdresser They had known Jess all their lives, she had worked in her mother's hairdresser's after she left school at sixteen in fact she had taken it over when her Mum retired and they had seen her around but now she seemed very different. She had the air of someone on a mission and this overwhelmed men's chauvinism and women's distrust of an ex hairdresser and made them want to spend time with her.

On the next Sunday, they went into Doncaster; she made them walk there as she said they would see more of life if they were on foot. Jess took them to the local Church, St Peter's in chains. After mass she went into the local hall and began to talk to the people, and many stayed on to hear her. They were surprised and even shocked by her words. She spoke directly, not in Church language or religious jargon that goes over people's heads. She spoke about the things that really matter to ordinary people and she did it with amazing confidence, no notes and no quotes, just straight from her heart.[2]

All of a sudden there was a commotion at the back of the hall. It was one of the local homeless men, an alcoholic, very disturbed. He started shouting and swearing at Jess. Moving forward through the crowd, frightening everyone. He screamed at the top of his voice:

'Why don't you just fuck off back to where you came from, I know you, you're another do gooder only interested in nice people, all words and no help for the likes of me.'

Jess walked towards the man, who was breathing heavily and bunching his fists, she led him to a seat in the front row, sat him down and began to talk to him. The man immediately became calm; Jess asked someone to make him a coffee and a sandwich. She spoke quietly to the man whilst all watched. Then she announced in a louder voice.

'This man is called Phil. He has suffered terribly in his life. He has become addicted to alcohol, but which one of you is not addicted to something? He has agreed to stay quiet and listen, and afterwards, he and I are going to talk some more and see if he can find a way out of the prison his life has become. Are you all okay with that?'

Most nodded or murmured their assent. They began whispering to each other: *'This is a new way of doing things, she talks about changing lives and then it starts, right in front of us. If she can cope with this guy what else can she do?'*

News Spreads News of this event got into the Advertiser, they interviewed Phil and some of the other people.[3] Jess had taken Phil to a rehab unit

---

[2] She called her method a sharing round. Wherever possible she had her listeners sit in a circle and invited them to respond to what she said from their hearts.

[3] This is where I came in; I was working as a freelance journalist for the Advertiser and sometimes for the Sheffield Star. They sent me to talk to Phil and check out the story.

and somehow persuaded them to take him on the spot. Phil was quoted as saying

'I don't know who that lass was but she has a kind of electricity coming out of her, when you're with her you begin to believe in yourself and that there is some power in her that can help you.'

Leaving the hall they took the bus back to Edlington (someone had given them a donation for food and travel); they went to the house of Rob and Andy, it was a terrace; third from the end of Baines Road. Joe and Julie went with them. Jess was introduced to Rob's family, his wife Bethany and the kids Nathan and Ryan. She was told that Bethany's Mum was really ill upstairs in bed, the Doctor was worried it might be pneumonia and was coming back in the morning to check on her.

Jess asked if she could see her, they took her up and Jess closed her eyes and laid hands on the woman's head and went very quiet. The woman who was called Shirley, in her late fifties stirred and then the colour came back to her cheeks. She told them she felt much better and would get up. Within half an hour she was downstairs making them something to eat and brewing a pot of tea!

Silent Healing Later, in the evening the door started to go and one after the other Rob and the others brought families in to see her in the front room. Sick kids, old folks with all kinds of ailments came and Jess made them better. Even very disturbed and addicted people, young lads hooked on glue and aerosols came and she seemed to get them all on the road to recovery. Though she told all of them to say nothing about what had happened. This went on late into the night.

While it was still dark, before dawn, she got up from the sofa she had slept on and went out of the house into the fields near old Edlington and sat wrapped in a blanket and was deeply silent. She sat that way for over an hour. When Rob and the others woke up and realised she had gone out they went looking for her. Having finally found her, annoyed they said; *'Everyone is searching for you'*.

But Jess answered *'Come on let's go to the other towns round here, Maltby, Askern, Rossington, Stainforth, I want to reach as many ordinary folk as I can.'*

She did the same as she had at St Peter's, talking about The Great Emergence, bringing recovery to people, helping the addicted, late into the night and up early to be alone, then off to the next place.

Infected by Prejudice A man in his late thirties, who was a haemophiliac and had contracted HIV from infected blood transfusions, came up to her in Rossington. He had been hounded out of his house because his neighbours accused him of being gay and feared he might infect them. He came up to Jess and took her aside, he begged her, insistently; *'I know that if you want to, you can help me'*.

Jess was really emotional, she put her arms around him, the man sobbed and sobbed, and then Jess put her hands around the face of the young man, looked into his eyes and said, *'I do want to help you, recover'*. Then she whispered so that only those close could hear, *'Say nothing to anyone but go to the Doncaster Royal Infirmary and ask them to test you for the virus, when you get a clear test this will show the people that you are better.'*

As soon as the man came back from the Hospital he told everyone he met what had happened. He would cut himself with a penknife and watch scabs form, because not only had his HIV vanished but his haemophilia had been cured as well.

So Jess had to keep away from the normal meeting places, for fear of being mobbed. She and her friends tried to keep themselves private and have time to eat and rest but people always found them, out on the crags or on the country roads. They were coming from all over now.

Back Home After a few weeks of this, Jess returned to Edlington, word quickly went round that she was home. She was in the house she grew up in with her family when people started coming.

They don't stand on ceremony in Edlington; they just knock and come in. One after the other they came, she didn't turn them away either, she shared her heart with them.

'Get Up Lad' The group got larger and larger pressing in at the door to hear her. Four men came to the gate carrying their mate on an old wooden door rigged up as a kind of stretcher. He had been injured in a pit accident years before and had gone from being in the local football team to weighing nearly forty stone, he was what the medical profession call *morbidly obese*.

They couldn't get him through the door; it took six of them to carry him, as his weight meant he had ceased to be able to walk. They began to take out the tip and turn window so they could manhandle him into the house that way. This all took about an hour and Jess was really taken aback by their tenacity and commitment to their comrade. Her family kicked up quite a fuss about the potential damage to the window, but Jess looked hard at the man now lying in front of her panting and weeping.

'Get up lad, and be released from this bondage in your body and from the trauma in your mind.'

One of the local health workers piped up, *'Hang on, we have been working with this guy for years and you think you can just wave a magic wand and cure him?'*

The local Vicar was also there with the Roman Catholic Parish priest. They also chipped in *'What do you mean by saying that you release him, only God can release people through the ministry of the Church'*.

The Catholic priest muttered, *'If he had come to mass once in a while it might have helped.'*

Jess heard these murmurings and she knew where they were coming from. *'Be careful, scepticism and self-protection will get in the way of the Great Emergence. Which is easier to say, be released or get up and get yourself off to hospital. But to show you that the Great Emergence is real . . .'* She now turned to the large bulk that was the man and said, *'Stand up, and lets call an ambulance so that they can take you to hospital and get you some proper treatment.'*

With all eyes on him the man did exactly that, he rolled over and with the help of his friends rose to his feet, standing in front of her unsteadily but resolutely. The ambulance was called and he waddled slowly out to it. He was treated and not a minute too soon, the doctors said his organs were giving out. He had a gastric band and lost nearly twenty-five stone. The people of the village became increasingly astonished at the change in the man.

Despised Jim and Dodgy Eddie Later that day, after yet another sharing round in the Miner's Welfare, Jess was walking through the town and she went into the local library where a Job Centre Plus event was on. She saw Jim Fitzgerald the manager of the Job Centre in Rotherham;

he was despised in the town for reporting benefit cheats, *spongers* as he called them. Many exploited the system just to pay for little extras for their kids, some to spend in the bookies, but they all hated Jim, even though he was an Edlington man and had worked down the pit. When Jess saw him she just said, *'Why don't you come and work with me now?'* Jim got up and left the office, there and then and went with her.

Later that day Jess and her mates were having their tea at the house of a man who was considered to have a foot on both sides of the law. He did a bit of poaching and sold drugs at his back door. He had been in prison for violence and had some pretty rough friends. Most in Edlington considered him a man to steer clear of. His name was Eddie Moss and Jess had met him because a couple of Eddie's cronies had spent a lot of time with Jess and become part of the group that went everywhere with her.

After they had eaten, they walked down to the Miner's Institute where the local vicar and the Church Warden took her to one side and said, *'What are you doing hanging round with these characters, they are criminals and bullies; they stole the lead off the church roof last year. We understand that you want to reach out to all sorts of people but have you thought about the kind of example you are setting to our parishioners and the good people who mind their own business and pay their taxes?'*

Jess came back at them quick as a flash,

'Who do you think goes to the doctor's, well people or those who know they need help? I am with those who know they need to change not those who think they have it sorted!'

To Drink or Not to Drink

There were many who had spent time with Rumi The Drowner and had learnt the value of not drinking alcohol and even sometimes fasting from food for a day every week to show solidarity with the poor. There were also some Muslim families in the area who were keeping

Ramadan, a period when they do not eat or drink in the hours of daylight. It also happened to have been Lent and some of the Church people had given up various luxuries for the period. Some of Jess's growing band of critics confronted her in the pub one lunchtime when she was talking with her group and others who had asked her to speak to them. One asked her, *'Why is it that most upright religious people are fasting in some way yet you are here drinking and enjoying yourself.'*

Jess gave it some thought and then answered

'If your favourite football team have just won the FA cup you don't sit around with long faces, you have a street party and everyone celebrates. As long as you are the cup winners you don't deprive yourselves. The time will come when the cup is given back and then they can start training again; and you can start denying yourselves and being sober. No one will take their best suit and cut it up to patch old jeans. The landlord here would not put his best bitter in old coke tins, no one would drink it and it would be wasted. The change I am talking about is something totally new!'

A Priest's Discomfort

Third Blog Edlington & The Peak District June-July 2011

It was Sunday and Jess and her friends had decided to go to mass in the Catholic Church. Some of the parishioners went to the Parish Priest and said,

'*She is not a Roman Catholic she should not receive communion here.*'

When Jess got to the Church, the Parish Priest, somewhat embarrassed, said to her before the service started:

'*Do you intend to take communion?*'

'*I do and so do my friends*'.

The priest looked over at the people who had reported Jess and shuffled uncomfortably in the pew.

'*You are not a Catholic are you?*'

'*No*' replied Jess '*I was christened in the Church of England up the road.*'

'*I am really sorry but I cannot let you take communion love, they will report me to the Bishop*'.

Jess stood up and to the great discomfort of the priest she got the attention of the whole congregation. She addressed them all,

'What do the words "take this all of you" mean to you. This is not a place where anyone should be excluded. Let me tell you the Great Emergence says that love is available to all; the only entry requirement is knowing your need for release and recovery.

'Sod Off'   In the back pew there was a man of the street who had sidled in as they were talking. He had a reputation for disrupting the Sunday Mass by pestering people for money and allowing his dog to wander round the church. Not many knew that he had been a soldier and an explosion in Iraq had caused him to lose his memory.

Jess went straight over to him as the parishioners tried to eject him out of the church as they had in the past. Jess said

'Do you know who you are friend?'

They said to her

'Don't bother with him he's disturbed, you can't help him, we often have to call the Police to remove him so we can get on with our mass in peace.' Jess said

'What is this mass about if it's not about caring for guys like this.'

She turned towards the man

'What is your name?'

The man replied

'Sod Off'.

Some of the mass goers told him off

'Don't talk like that in Church, go on, get out'.

Jess however understood.

'Is that what every one says to you, is that why you call yourself Sod Off?'

The man brightened

'Yes, you see I can't remember my real name.'

'He's just a malingerer'

One of the congregation muttered, another said,

'He seems to have enough to feed that mongrel, so why does he keep bothering us?'

Jess was angry now; she pulled the man called '*Sod Off*' to one side into the chapel where the font was.

He began to stir the water,

'*Hey leave that alone*' said someone else '*that's holy water, not for the likes of you, look at him he doesn't even wash!*'

Jess ignored them

'*Do you want to remember, it might be painful?*'

The man nodded slowly. Jess took some of the water in both hands and poured it over the man's head, and then she took another handful and let the dog drink it. The man looked dazed and then needed to sit down. After a few minutes he looked up at Jess and said:

'*Michael, that's my name, I was a paratrooper. We found a mine and then . . .*'

He began to weep and Jess put her arms round him, he howled with pain and grief for a long time, about twenty minutes. People tutted and scolded them demanding that they leave so they could get on with the mass. Jess finally lifted the man and led him out and said over her shoulder as she left,

'*What is church for if not the cure of hearts and minds like Michael's.*'

The Parish priest stayed in church for a long time after mass. Those who had initially complained about him went home and rang the bishop.

Peace and Crowds

Jess did what she had always done when she wanted peace; she got on a bus and headed for the Peak District. Her comrades went with her. The trouble was that her reputation had grown and hundreds of people from the Doncaster and Rotherham areas wanted to check her out for themselves.

Some of the crowd were from Sheffield so far had the talk of her and her activities spread. She had to sit on top of a large rock on Higgar Tor[4] so that the press of the crowd wouldn't trample her. Before she spoke to them she touched, listened to and anointed many people. She used water and oil to help her soothe and heal people and she listened to those who were very disturbed or addicted. Many of the latter sensed there was a power in her but she made a point of forbidding them to talk to anyone about it. She would say

'Just go and seek recovery, quietly, no fuss',

At points her friends were scared that she would be crushed by the sheer amount of people pushing and shoving. Many said she was good with oils and the like because she had been in the beauty business but the effects were far more profound.

After that they walked over to Edale and climbed Jacob's Ladder going up onto Kinder Scout.[5] She only took up those who she wanted to be her closest comrades. She chose a dozen of them to go up with her.

Ambassadors She told them to be her ambassadors, none of them were highly educated, and one of them finally plucked up the courage to ask what on earth she meant by ambassadors. She said that they would be given the chance to be her apprentices, to learn her trade, that of curing hearts and minds and to begin the Great Turning. They were to go out and tell people about the Great Emergence and would have the power to begin the recovery process in people, but first they must go through the Great Change themselves.

These are the people she chose.

- Rob Stuart (Jess gave him the nickname 'Solid')
- Jeff and Julie Marsh (Jess nicknamed them the 'Fire-Starters')

---

[4] Higgar Tor is a large outcrop in the Peak District near Sheffield very popular with Climbers.

[5] A large, high escarpment between Manchester and Sheffield.

- Andy Green (Rob's Best Mate)
- Eddie Moss (A small time criminal who on meeting Jess had begun to change his ways)
- Bethany Philips (A foster mother who was between children)
- Jim Fitzgerald (The Job Centre Manager)
- Tim Menzies (A computer nerd who lived with his parents, he spent his time mending people's machines for beer money)
- Josie Shepherd (The daughter of a local authority councillor who was in disgrace because he had been convicted of embezzling money, Josie was also on the dole.)
- Bounty Treasure (An Afro-Caribbean woman who drove buses and had been attacked by a passenger and was off work with post traumatic stress)
- Kumar Ahmed (A Bangladeshi from Rotherham who had been arrested for suspected terrorist activities, he was released because nothing could be proved)
- Davina Carroll (A young woman who had worked with Jess)

Having chosen her team she took them back home to Edlington.

Delusions of Grandeur As had become the norm, crowds gathered every time she went to a public place, this happened so often that they hardly had a minute to grab a bite to eat. When her family and relations saw this all going on they appeared one morning, just as she was about to run a sharing round.

'*We are taking you home*' they said, '*and we aren't taking no for answer. This is mad you are getting into deep water here, we all think you have delusions of grandeur. We want to have you sectioned*'

But she ignored them and they were unable to make her go with them because the crowd loved her and would have become ugly if they had tried to manhandle her, so she continued her work.

Shades of the Occult   An ecumenical[6] group of clergymen were sent by the authorities in London to investigate the whole matter (so far had news of her spread). When they had been there for a while a local TV news team interviewed them.

'*Where do you think this woman gets her powers from?*' asked the reporter.

'*We think that she is using some form of hypnotism learnt from those New Age people she was meant to have spent time with, when she kept going to Derbyshire. She is into all the New Age crazes, someone told us she uses Tarot Cards and Crystal healing. If you open yourself to unknown forces you are more than likely involved with the occult. We know there are covens who worship the devil at the stone circles in the Peak District.*'

The news team went straight to Jess with this story,

'*People are saying you derive your power from contact with a witches coven that you encountered in Derbyshire, that you have got yourself caught up with the occult. That is how you are effecting these cures of the addicted and the disturbed*'.

Jess smiled,

'*Can I tell you a story?*'

They nodded hoping for a good sound-bite to put on TV that evening. But she insisted they turn the cameras off before she spoke.

'*In order to deal with a Mafia family would the police employ another Mafia family to get rid of them? Surely not because, once the first family was ousted from all its protection rackets the new one would take them over and the situation would be even worse. Even if they all killed each other another family would be quick to move in. No, you have to get to the roots of evil. Let me put it another*

---

6   From different church denominations

way; the only way to steal from a millionaire is to tie him up and disable all his alarm systems, get the combination for his safe then you can get to his valuables.'

They looked confused.

'So are you and your followers are trying to take over the Church, is that what you are saying?'

She replied, 'No, the evil force I am dealing with here is all the things that imprison the human spirit, that is the force I want to disable.'

'The clergy from London say you are doing it with occult powers, are you?' The reporter was tenacious.

'You go back and tell them this. There is nothing that can be done or said that cannot be forgiven, but when you start confusing your own biased and self serving judgements with the will of God you are in danger of creating God in your own image and that God will never forgive anyone. Those who see evil in goodness are in a prison that goodness cannot free them from.' This left the reporters utterly perplexed and when they reported her words on television, the Church authorities were furious.

Jess's immediate family turned up again. They did not come into the hall where she was; they sent a message in that they needed to talk to her outside. The message was passed to her,

'Your mother and brothers are outside and want to talk to you.'

Jess looked around at the group she was with and said

'You are all my mother and my brothers and sisters, my family. Anyone who decides to be part of the Great Turning is a member of my family.'

Great Stories— Great Change She went back into the centre of Doncaster; the weather was good, so she gathered a crowd outside the Frenchgate Centre. There were so many that she had to stand on one of the benches to be seen. To be heard, she used a loud hailer. She told many stories to illustrate what the Great Change was about.

An African Emergency *'Listen'* she said. *'A charity raising money for the third world sent out an email for its latest African Drought appeal.*

Some of the people, receiving the emails saved them to their to do list but then forgot about them. Some replied immediately and enthusiastically but then failed to fill in the direct debit attachment and soon forgot all about it. Others did not notice the communication among all their junk mail or they got a computer virus and lost all their data, whatever happened nothing came of the email. Some others told everyone all about the email and were put off by their friends saying that all the money they gave would go towards the Charity workers wages and office costs and hardly any of it would reach Africa. But some read it and sent money, lots of money and the famine was averted. Let anyone who has their wits about them hear this and do something about the Great Turning!'

Why Stories? When they left Doncaster those who were on the bus with her asked about the story she had told. She said this to them

'Look the Great Turning is really hard for people to grasp straight away. So I use stories that if you think about them long enough they become like a wedge that gradually opens up a chink, then a crack and then a chasm.

But with you I try to be straight because you are on the journey with me and have seen the Great Change in action. To the others I want to keep it simple and in story form so they can grasp it instinctively. The trouble is those who think they are clever feel above such stories and ignore them as if it were beneath their intelligence'

'Do you understand the story of the email?' they looked blankly at her, 'The email is the message of the Great Turning, the ones who save the email and then forget are those who hear me and are initially enthusiastic but then quickly lose their excitement and are never seen again; I call them people pleasers who please no one, not even themselves.

The ones who respond but fail to make the donation are those who sign up for the Turning and start the process but then it gets too hard and they sidle off.

The ones who have lots of junk mail or viruses are those who think that the message of the Great Change is just one idea among many and lose it in the clutter of their good intentions, or those with a virus are those who allow the constant stimulation of the entertainment on offer, TV, games, mobile phones, the internet, constant relationships with no depth, anything addictive, to suffocate their deep desires.

The one's who allow themselves to be persuaded out of the Great Change are those who cannot find any drive in *themselves, who cannot be alone and silent so trade their true selves for the opinion and esteem of others and this enslaves them.*

Those who sent the money are the ones who sense the Great Emergence and are in touch with their deep desire for it, they may not be strong but they are honest about their pain and losses and they embrace the Turning. They sort out their lives and in doing so become agents of hope in the world, without ever trying to fix anyone else.'

Only as Sick as your Secrets

Then she said *'Does anyone buy a new Flat Screen TV and put it in a cupboard so that no one can see it. No, you put in a place where the whole family can watch it. So with the Change nothing is kept hidden, it is brought into view so that it can be dealt with, you are only as sick as your secrets!*

Look Out For Number One

'Are you hearing me, are you able to really listen? Beware those who say you have to be cruel to be kind; it is dog eat dog; look out for number one. The Emergence turns this dead logic on its head. Trust the giving instinct in you, help others and you will be helping yourself, do not become judge, jury and executioner because you will install them in the courtroom of your heart and one day the defendant will be you and you will find the same rough justice you offered to others.'

Golden Trumpets

Jess had another image for the Great Emergence, *'It is like a gardener who buys a whole load of bulbs in autumn and plants them all over her garden. All through the winter nothing happens the ground is cold and dead. Then the spring comes and the tiny green shoots protrude from the earth. Then the full plant grows up and then finally the beautiful yellow trumpets of a multitude of daffodils. She did nothing except have faith in the cold earth that it would* grow the bulbs. She fills her house with the blooms and they bring her great joy.'*

She went on *'How can I tell you all about this Great Turning, Great Search, Great Change, Great Emergence, Great Peace?*

Can You See the Tree in the Seed? *It is like the acorn; many fall from the Oak in autumn and are lost but one or two seed themselves. Then over hundreds of years the seedling becomes this huge and enduring tree. Can you see the great oak in the acorn? No and yet one leads to the other.'*

Her sharing was full of images, even her words; Great Search, Great Change, Great Peace, Great Emergence and Great Turning were images. She fitted her stories to her audience trying to find pictures from everyday life and not go over their heads. When she was alone with her friends she went back over the days talk and tried to expand and give them the bigger picture.

Vulnerability as Strength Late one evening, in Sheffield, as they were waiting in the bus station to get back to Edlington they heard the noise of a great crowd of people coming towards them. Jess was asleep on a bench she was exhausted. The crowd were opposing football fans coming away from a match; they were rampaging down the road fighting. Anyone who got in the way was caught up in it. They were using baseball bats and knives, throwing bricks and smashing windows, many were hurt and injured.

The Police were trying to contain it but to no avail. They were coming straight towards Jess and her comrades. She stayed asleep, they were terrified and ready to run, but they could not wake her. Finally they managed to stir her. *'Jess, look we are going to get hurt, come on let's run'.*

She woke up looked at the rioting crowd coming towards them and held up her arms. '*Stop, calm down, for everybody's sake, give it a rest.'*

She cut a small but determined figure against the crowd, and she spoke in the most commanding voice. Something about her, the strength of her vulnerability, stopped the mob in its tracks and they immediately settled down. Everyone began to disperse as if nothing had happened. She turned to her friends, '*why do you doubt the love that is looking after you, fear is your enemy not people, have some trust.'*

As they got on the bus they said to each other

'*Who is this woman? That was awesome, she was so calm and cool, and where did she learn how to do that?*

*A Man & a Village
All Tied Up*

Jess and her comrades travelled by train to Bamford to spend time out in the hills by staying at the campsite there. As they got off the train they walked into an uproar. The people of the village had heard she was coming and were congregating around the platform, keen to see her and hear her words.

Fifth Blog Bamford & Sheffield July-September 2011

A man from the village had travelled on the same train. He jumped out of the carriage and ran towards Jess shouting, swearing and gesticulating wildly at the villagers. Some of the men ran towards him and restrained him, others called the Police to come and take him away. Jess asked what the man's story was.

'Oh he's as mad as a stag that one'. Someone said.

It emerged that the man had grown up in the village and on his eighteenth birthday he had come out as being gay. His family could not or would not deal with this and he took the rejection badly. He began to travel to Sheffield regularly going to gay clubs; he got a flat there but he could not accept being ostracised by his family, so every so often he would return to try and persuade them accept his life choices. He then contracted HIV generating even more animosity from his family and a growing number of the villagers. He would come out and pitch a tent at the local campsite and confront his family and others in the village.

He became increasingly depressed and fell into taking heroin, he was now thin and gaunt. Recently he had been banned from the campsite and would sleep in the cemetery and harangue people from behind the gravestones. He ran out one day when his Father was passing and grabbed him to make him talk to him. His Father fell and broke his arm. The family took out an injunction against their son to prevent him from coming near them.

On another occasion he tried again, this time hammering on his parent's door until his Mother let him in. His returning Father told him to leave so he flew into a rage smashing up the house until the Police were called to restrain him. The family finally and reluctantly had him sectioned, forcibly removing him to a mental health unit in Sheffield. But that very day he had escaped and come out on the same train as Jess.

Suddenly he managed to get free of his captors and threw himself at Jess before anyone could stop him. He grabbed at her shouting,

'What are you doing coming to this village, I know who you are; you are that Jess everyone is on about. Are you yet another bitch who is going to send me away, I bet you are, you sanctimonious cow'

Jess had become very still and poised she reached towards him and held the man by the shoulders.

'What do they call you?' Jess asked.

'The other patients call me Riot, because I cannot control myself, my feelings take over and trouble seems to follow me wherever I go.'

Jess produced a bottle of Frankincense oil and said to the man called 'Riot',

'Do you want to be released from this hell?'

He replied *'Yes but I don't want to be a zombie like when I am on the drugs the hospital make me take'*.

The police had arrived at that point but they couldn't reach the man, as the crowd around Jess was so deep. They were next to a field that had a large flock of sheep grazing in it. Jess said,

'Look if I can make the feelings go away but still allow you to be who you really are, would you want that?'

The man was beginning to shake and a fit of anxiety was coming over him, he needed a fix and was going into a cold sweat.

'I would give anything to be free of this', he said through clenched teeth.

Jess began to anoint him and to put her hands on his head, the man called Riot acted as if an electric shock had gone through him, he went rigid and then slumped to the ground, he let out a scream like an express train going into a tunnel. The sheep in the adjacent field panicked and ran as one, straight at the crowd which had to jump out of the way, the whole flock spilled straight onto the main road and hurtled off. They caused no end of hold ups as they ran throughout the area; many of them were lost and never seen again.

When the crowd re-gathered around Jess they were astonished to see the man called Riot sitting cross-legged on the floor talking to Jess in his right mind. He no longer looked pale and haunted and Jess was talking to him about the process of recovery.

'Stopping taking drugs is only the first stage, you need to go to a group I know in Sheffield, called Narcotics Anonymous, they will help you to stay clean. I have helped relieve your body you need to work on your heart and mind.'

Many in the crowd urged the Police to arrest the man and take him back to hospital but he spoke with quiet assurance,

'Its okay, I am going back on the train, allow me the dignity of walking back on to the ward of my own accord.'

He was so lucid and obviously sane that the Police agreed. The crowd then turned on Jess and her company,

'Get away from here, you have meddled enough, can't you see how much you have upset this man's family'.

The local vicar ushered them back on to the next train,

'Please don't come back' he said *'we are good people here and we do not need your theatrics, that man has caused no end of trouble to his family and your interfering has just made things worse. I tried to counsel him for years but there are some people you just cannot help, maybe you'll learn that one-day. More to the point the farmer will want compensation for his livestock and obviously none of you can afford it, go on, just go, leave us to get on with our lives.*

As she was getting back on to the train the man who had been cured ran up to Jess and begged her to allow him to join her group.

'No' said Jess, *'I told you go and get clean, then carry the message to others, what I have done for you, you can do for others, people will get clean because of you.'*

The man that had been called Riot did just that and went around the towns in the High Peak and beyond seeking out addicts and helping them to go on the Great Search, to face up to their need for change and to find the Great Peace. Many families were put back together by his work, in fact I interviewed some of them, his results were astonishing.

Two Desperate Cases The train arrived back into Sheffield and already there was a great crowd in the station forecourt. The Archdeacon of Sheffield, someone fairly well placed in the Church of England pushed his way through to the front of the crowd, his name was the Reverend Jeremy Parker, and he was 46 years old. He actually fell to his knees before Jess begging,

'My little girl is dying in the Children's Hospital, please come and lay your hands on her and keep her alive'.

The tears were running down his cheeks and people were amazed that Jess also immediately began to weep and agreed to go with him. As they walked up through the crowded city streets more and more people followed, as those near Jess told others that she might be about to do something extraordinary!

A woman heard the commotion and realised who it was walking past. She had suffered for years with female incontinence, it had ruined her life as she constantly reeked of urine and she ended up living alone because her condition revolted her family. She had spent everything she had trying to find a cure, but no amount of private medicine or alternative therapy had worked, she just became poorer and more unwell.

She had heard about Jess already and decided that if only she could touch her she might find a cure. As the crowd came to a bottleneck in the underpass she slipped in behind her and grasped Jess's hand. She immediately felt a return of bladder control and she knew it had worked. At the same time Jess sensed an energy leaving her.

'*Who touched me?*' she demanded.

Her friends looked at her as if she were losing it. Bethany said:

'*Come on Jess there must be a few hundred people in this underpass all pushing and shoving, loads of them have touched you!*'

Yet Jess kept asking and in the end the woman stepped forward and again she knelt down in front of her and told her what had happened. Jess looked at her amazed,

'*Your willingness to trust your instinct has saved you, you are cured, go and I hope your life improves.*'

As she was saying this to the woman, the Archdeacon's secretary came towards them; she took the Cleric aside as the crowd looked on. She told him that his daughter had just died and that his wife wanted him back at the hospital as soon as possible.

Jess realised by his face what must have happened and walked over to them. She said, '*Don't be scared by this death, believe in the Great Peace*'.

She strode off and reached the hospital entrance, she would not let anyone go inside with her apart from Rob, Jeff and Julie. They followed the Archdeacon to the ward, when they arrived the whole family was there, beside themselves with grief.

The intensive care unit was very still, all the staff subdued in the presence of death. She looked at them all and said,

'Why are you all so distraught? This child is not beyond our help, she will return'.

The family were deeply insulted by her words and the staff wanted to eject her and her people. But the Archdeacon would not let them and led Jess to the bed with the girl on it. They drew the curtains around the girl and her Mother. Jess lent over the girl and breathed on her,

'Up you get little one' she whispered.

The girl opened her eyes and the breath returned to her lungs, she sat up and stared at Jess with a look of one who has been called back from the edge of a cliff, both relieved and surprised. The girl was twelve years of age; Jess demanded that all the tubes be removed and that she be made comfortable. They drew the curtains and the staff could not believe their eyes. Jess told them to give her some food and something to drink. She told them that what had occurred was confidential and they should respect the privacy of the family by telling no one.

Unappreciated at Home

She left Sheffield straight away and returned to Edlington, with her friends. That Sunday she gave a sharing at the Miners Institute, many of them had never heard her speak, they were impressed.

'*This lass can talk*' they said, '*how did a woman from Edlo get to be so clever?*'

But others, though they were impressed had read the recent article in the Advertiser that week, saying that Jess had not completed her hairdressing qualifications, they had interviewed her brother and sisters who were all bemused by her antics.

'*She thinks she's so clever but she's just one of us, and now she's telling us how to live, I don't think so.*'

'*I was at school with her she was worse than me at RE*' one of them said and most agreed.

Jess said to them

'*Artists are rarely appreciated by their own families or the critics, many writers were not recognised by the people they grew up with, it seems impossible that an ordinary person might be able to see things in a new way!*'

Sixth Blog
Edlington,
Armthorpe,
Askern,
Stainforth,
Moorlands,
Maltby,
Catcliffe,
Brinsworth,
Treeton &
Sheffield
September-
October
2011

34

She was unable to perform any of the changes she had in other places. She touched a few of the ill and troubled and they got better, but she could do no more, so she left. She couldn't fathom the way they treated her, as she loved her hometown. Bemused she made the rounds of the surrounding area, Armthorpe, Rossington, Askern, even Stainforth and Moorlands.

Out in Pairs One morning Jess gathered her friends in the local café in Edlington. Sending them out in pairs she said, *'You have seen me set addicts on the road to recovery; you have watched me change and set free, go and do the same thing.'*

She continued

'Don't take a whole lot of stuff with you; you won't need anything except what I have given you, the message of the Great Turning. No fundraising, no gimmicks, just do what you have seen me do. Stay with the people, don't expect special treatment just what they can offer you. If folk don't take you seriously and don't take any notice, no problem just move on to the next place.'

So they set off, working in different places, they went as far as Barnsley and Rotherham, Sheffield and Chesterfield. They set a great many addicts on the road to recovery; they spoke powerfully of the Great Turning and the Great Peace that came from it. Many sick and infirm people were changed and wherever they stayed the night and were made welcome, that house became a much better place.

Media Silence Barry Priestly the Leader of Sheffield City Council heard about the events surrounding Jess, it was hard not to, they began to appear in the Star, South Yorkshire's local Newspaper. The work of Jess and her followers had become a favourite topic among local journalists. However the press could never get interviews with her or her comrades and they always told those they met to keep their work secret.

The local radio stations were beginning to try and get hold of her or those who had experienced some change because of Jess and her work. Jess kept herself to herself and away from the press, however some could not resist the lure of five minutes of fame. She said the message spread more honestly by word of mouth.

Snuffing out the Truth

Priestly said to his cronies
'This has to be something to do with that Jalaladin Rumi, perhaps he told her to come and haunt me.'

One of his advisers said,
'No she is more like a suffragette, a radical, someone hell bent on upsetting the status quo!'

Another said
'She reminds me of Aung San Suu Kyi from Burma with all this non-violence crap, and look at the trouble she's caused, we need to watch her, she could be a problem. There is an election coming up and she might turn people against us'

But Priestly was adamant
'No it's that lunatic Rumi, we got rid of him but somehow here he is influencing her from beyond the grave!'

Barry Priestly had done away with the man who had started it all out in the brooks around Grindleford. Jalaladin Rumi had begun to criticise the way the city was being run, lots of big, high profile projects that gained kudos for the councillors and great share options in the companies that built them. Priestly knew he would have a few company directorships waiting for him when he stood down as leader.

Rumi had asked very public questions about all this. He had demanded to know how it helped those who were still living in rubbish housing stock and trapped in poverty.

When Sheffield made a bid to host the commonwealth games this was the last straw for Barry. The wild man, *Rumi* made it a point to speak out about the bid on every possible occasion. The more people that came out to experience the drowning of their old lives, the more the word went round about his denouncements of the bid, he criticised the free trips to other countries to see how they had hosted the games, the parties and the expense accounts.

'*Barry Priestley and his cronies are on expense accounts whilst many in this city do not have enough to feed their kids or a decent roof over their heads.*'

At the time the Commonwealth Committee came to the city Jalaladin Rumi organised a week of fasting and prayer. Asking people to wear a yellow garment in solidarity with him and to collect the money they saved to give to a charity that built affordable housing in the city.

Now this infuriated Barry's wife Carla, she loved the power and prestige that went with being married to the Leader of the Council, she was certainly encouraging Barry to lobby for Sheffield to have an elected Mayor with far more power. She was even beginning to think how they could move on to positions of greater influence.

Rumi's *week of fasting* was just too much for her, mainly because it was so effective; the Commonwealth Committee were asking very awkward questions. What upset her most was that although her husband seemed to hate the Sufi Teacher as much as she did, he also had a peculiar and fearful fascination for him.

Carla Priestly with the help of a tame journalist finally unearthed that when Jalaladin Rumi had been Jed Patterson he had visited Afghanistan and spent time in a *Madrasa* with alleged connections to the Taliban. She had the rumour spread that he had gone from there to a terrorist training camp. She had the story blown up and implied that he was really a terrorist with anti western tendencies. She kept at it and finally Barry gave in and persuaded the Police to arrest him using anti terror legislation.

This took him off the streets for the end of the committee's visit and discredited him with many of the people, though a significant minority of the city still wore the yellow garment and campaigned for his release.

What infuriated Carla even more was that Barry would go to the cells where Jalaladin Rumi was being held and have long talks with him. Barry knew in his heart of hearts that keeping him locked up was wrong but he felt trapped between his conscience and his ambitions. Carla arranged on the last night of the committee's visit for Barry and a couple of the delegates to be visited by some high class escorts, Barry got very drunk and the escorts had been instructed to dress the men up in leather gear and then photograph the proceedings.

The next day Carla confronted Barry with the pictures. She said that if he did not arrange for Rumi to be deported to Afghanistan she would make them public so much did she hate the man. She knew that Barry would give in as he valued his power too much and he also knew she would find a way to stay in charge without him such was her ambition.

So he finally persuaded the chief of South Yorkshire Police to quietly have Jalaladin Rumi deported. Some of his followers tried to find him after the deportation but were unable to locate him. The rumour was that he had been assassinated somewhere on the Pakistan-Afghanistan border, although no one could say who had done it.

Food from Nowhere

Jess's comrades, those sent out to work returned and told her about all that they had achieved, and the effect on the people. The message of the Great Turning had travelled as far as Manchester and Scunthorpe, Leeds and Nottingham. People had been transformed and were transforming others. Jess took them to a place near Maltby called Roche Abbey.

'*Lets get some space, you all need a rest*'.

They took a barbecue with them, as they had no time on the road even to eat a meal and had grabbed food where they could. Someone saw them get off the bus in Maltby and word went round as to where they were headed. Many arrived before them and still more followed so that by the time they got settled there was a huge crowd. The English

Heritage employee who looked after the ruin just let them all in without charge, so many were there. Jess looked around and felt very sorry for the them all, they were so desperate to listen to her, they had rushed out of their houses, coming as they were, still more arriving all the time.

She shared for an hour or so and then broke for questions, she seemed to have the knack of putting another question that touched the heart of the questioner and led them to their own answers. After that the people came for healing and listening work. Her friends also healed and listened, now that they had learned from her the way to open people to the Great Emergence. This went on all afternoon and into the evening. Some of her companions took her aside during a break and said,

'Look Jess, we are at least two miles from the nearest chippy, there are too many people, send them home or to Maltby to get something to eat.'

'You feed them' she replied.

They looked at each other, utterly confused.

'What, we don't have enough of our own food and we certainly don't have the money to go and buy takeaways for all this lot.'

'What food have you got?' she said.

'Just what we bought for the barbecue' they said.

'Okay get it going and I will get the people to sit down in groups'.

She did this and when she came back the food was cooking nicely, the smell was filling the whole valley.

She stretched her hands over the food and honoured it for its power to sustain life:

'May this food be a sign of the abundance of the Great Peace' she said.

'Right, I want you to start giving it out to the groups nearest to us.'

They began tentatively, convinced it would run out, but it didn't, each group had enough, more than enough.

They were not sure what happened, did people begin to share what they had with them or did the food they cooked just multiply? Every time the barbecue was emptying more food was found together with more charcoal. Whatever happened, there were piles of leftovers and many took food home with them, including Jess's friends. There must have been close to a thousand people in the valley that evening and they were all fed.

A Fight Averted   As soon as they had finished eating Jess insisted that her friends start walking to Catcliffe, as she wanted to speak to people in the towns around Sheffield.

It was already getting dark and she said she wanted to stay in that holy place and be still for a while, she told them she would catch them up. They walked to the main road and the last bus came so they decided to take it.

It was full of people who had come out of the pubs, going to Sheffield for the nightclubs. Drink fuelled arguments were happening all over the bus; Jess's friends were being drawn into them. The Bus Driver stopped the bus and was demanding some kind of order, this went on for a good hour and things were about to get seriously out of hand, the driver was on the verge of calling the police. Suddenly they realised that Jess had appeared on the bus and was moving from group to group, calm seemed to spread wherever she went. Then she said to her friends

'Why didn't you walk like I asked, it's a good job I noticed you, I was going to walk by. But the Great Peace was needed here and you are still so inexperienced that you couldn't cope.'

She looked around and said

'Lets get off this bus and take in the night air'.

They followed her stunned. They were all scared by the events of day and night, what was it they were caught up in?

As soon as they arrived in Catcliffe the sun was rising and shops were beginning to open and people were out and about. Word went around very quickly that Jess was there. They opened up the local hall and she went to work sharing with the people. Then they brought her many who were in need of healing. She listened to them and recovery of minds and bodies began for all of them. She proceeded to visit the towns in that area, Brinsworth, Treeton and many others.

She was becoming very well known, often the local media interviewed those whom she had touched or listened to and they were all consistent in their testimony that something came out of her that empowered them to make changes in their lives. They did not feel in any way judged rather they felt totally accepted and able to rediscover some inner sense of self-worth and a road to recovery. Jess herself always refused to be interviewed and counselled her friends to do the same. This only fascinated the media more; in fact she was starting to show up on the radar of the national press.

A Fact Finding Mission

Jess was also attracting the attention of the religious authorities, the Catholic and Anglican Bishops, along with the Methodists, had set up a joint committee to enquire into her work. A team of clergy and lay people were dispatched on a fact-finding mission, following her around and gathering evidence.

This team immediately noted that neither Jess nor her comrades regularly attended any church; she would conduct sharing rounds in different churches, but they were too busy dealing with the crowds to attend Sunday services. Even more disturbing to the Fact-Finders was that they would sometimes go to a Mosque, a Sikh Gurdwara or a Buddhist centre. The team decided to seek a meeting with her, so she invited them to a local pub in Catcliffe and when all were seated she encouraged their questions, however what came back at her were statements.

The first from an Anglican Clergyman, *'We are very concerned about your popularity and the kind of example you are setting to all these unchurched people. You are going to confuse them if you do not stick to one church, they will think it is okay to just pick and choose parishes, denominations even religions!'*

The second from a Catholic Monsignor; *'You go to communion[7] all over the place and a number of your followers don't even seem to be Christian. These actions undermine many of the truths of the Christian faith. By all means visit different temples and centres but don't act as if they are equal to ours!'*

Jess looked them full in the face.

A Tirade *'I have spent a lot of time watching the way you all carry on and it strikes me as very true that your religion has provided you with the safest place to hide from God.*

It is clear to me that if you make your churches a safe harbour to shelter from the harsh realities of people's daily existence, you end up more interested in maintaining the harbour than looking after those in danger on the high seas of life.

If you make attending services a condition for acceptance and a measure of worthiness, then going to church on Sunday seems enough; but that means you care nothing about the quality of awakening for the rest of the week.

If you care nothing about facing what is real, nothing about how to be part of the Great Turning, how to become an agent of the Great Peace; if you care nothing that we all, whether we go to church or not, have immediate access to what you call God just because we are all human beings; if you say nothing about dying in order to live, then you've truly missed the point!

And all the while you make religion a prison for your people and for your own souls, a place of duty not freedom, a place for doctrines and laws, not transformation.

---

[7]   Consuming Bread and Wine

There are pockets of the Great Turning in some Churches but mostly you've made a system out of the tree of life, leaching the sap and poisoning the roots, rotting the trunk, the branches have withered, as has any chance of new growth. The Great Turning is for everyone not just those who subscribe to your system!

Even worse the higher you climb to the top of your Churches the more you've to lie to yourself that what is on offer is real freedom; and so you just stop asking the questions that really matter and seek to protect your own position or treat being honest and open as an evil, let me tell you **that is** the real lie.'

She was really warming to her theme now,

'You Catholics, you heard the words of Jesus "take this all of you" *about the bread and wine and instead of giving it freely, to all, you have made it a way of excluding the broken, and for what, so that you all stay more pure? That is not purity it is exclusion and exclusion in the name of God!*

None of your churches are very good at this, you all do the same thing; you forget that mercy is the heart of the Great Change and want to force your people to fit a blueprint that many of you don't even stick to yourselves; it is not about making people into something but helping them to accept who they already are, which is nothing short of miraculous. You can't see the Great Emergence because of the Church shaped glasses you all wear and they filter out most of the signs that the Turning is happening all around you.

The people in the pub were looking on and wondering what she was talking about,

'Look' she said 'at all these faces looking at you, we are all searching, all of us, for what this life is all about.'

She turned to the mass of locals and said

'It is not what building you go to on Sunday or Friday or Saturday or any other day of the week that matters, it is what you give your life for, what you spend your precious time on that tells you what you are really all about.

Your life is astonishing and everything you do with it means something, so do something you can feel was worth being on the planet for.

I tell you the world we live in is utterly shining with its own light but hardly anyone takes the time to cast their shadow over the ground and see their own outline.'

They left the pub and went back to the house of a woman known for her community work, she wasn't a churchgoer but she liked what Jess was saying.

Jess's friends were perplexed and asked what she meant at the end about the light and the shadow.

She said

'Look most people live unconscious lives, and they never ask what this all means, they are drugged by all the distractions, TV, drink, debts, scapegoating, addictions of all kinds, and those with the message of transformation don't even realise what they have. They make their Churches into self-serving clubs but do nothing to offer ordinary people any sense of what all this means—that life is the greatest adventure you can be on. It is because they haven't realised it for themselves that they can't help anyone else to see it.

Church goers can be like people sitting on a gold mine but not realising it, yet unwilling to let anyone else try and dig for gold.'

The Fact-Finding Team left the pub seething with indignation; no one had ever spoken to them like that before.

A Traveller's Cheek She left Catcliffe and decided to take her friends on the train from Sheffield to Cleethorpes to get away from things for a while. They booked themselves into a bed and breakfast, the money came from the donations many people made to her cause, most of which she gave away to those in need. As they were walking along the front and talking to each other about everything they had witnessed, a Traveller woman who was selling lucky heather grabbed Jess's coat and stopped her saying:

'I have the sight and I have seen in the cards that you are a holy woman. You can't fool me, I can see it shining out of you lady. My daughter is afflicted, she is addicted to crack, a terrible thing, we cannot get her off it. You can help her, you know you can, will you please miss, please miss.'

'Well sister' she said *'do you think I came to this place just to look after your type who most folk think are just parasites scrounging off good upright people'*

Jess had a kind of glint in her eye that those who were close to her knew. She had it when she nicknamed the siblings Jeff and Julie the Fire-Starters as they were always up for a fight. The woman came back at Jess like a shot.

'If you don't care for us then what chance do we have, only God has ever been interested in us? They used to put up notices in the pubs in this town, saying 'No Travellers' and even now when they daren't put up the signs they makes it obvious, we aren't wanted, never will be.'

Jess smiled *'For that answer, know that the recovery of your daughter has begun, go back and find her, if she trusts you she will never be in the grip of crack again.'*

The heather seller went back to her camp immediately and found her daughter burning all her drugs on a brazier with a smile on her face.

Prisons or Cocoons They took the train back to Doncaster and Jess travelled all around that area going to the villages and towns. In the Frenchgate shopping centre she was talking to a large crowd when a young couple led a man to her who was suffering from depression, he had been in and out of psychiatric wards, taken all kinds of medication, he was gaunt and broken. Jess took him to one side and listened to him, and then said to the man,

Eighth Blog
Peak District,
Maltby,
Wickersly,
Denaby Main,
Harrogate,
Wetherby,
Spofforth,
Knaresborough
January-
March
2012

'This prison you have been in is not a jail, it is a cocoon and I want you to emerge from it now and live again'

Something in the listening and Jess's words released the man. He fell into Jess's arms weeping and Jess handed him over to the couple (his niece and her husband) and she said to them.

'Listen your Uncle isn't crazy, he just couldn't live with the madness of our society, you can help him to live differently, by living differently yourselves.'

Jess asked them to tell no one about what had happened, that it was confidential but the more she said these things the more people talked and were amazed at everything she did and said.

'She does everything well, no matter who comes to her she seems to understand what they need.'

More and more pieces about her *More Food From Nowhere* appeared in the media and one local paper called it the 'Jess Phenomenon'. They tried to get her to appear on local TV and radio but she always turned them down.

A month or so later they travelled back to the Peak District to the area around Hathersage. Someone had lent them a couple of vans that they now used to get around. Jess liked to get out into the wilder country and draw people out of the cities and towns. She had attracted about four thousand people, mainly men as she had some important things to teach them about themselves and their journey through life.

Many were amazed at this, as very few men were interested in religion anymore. But they hung off her every word and gesture. Women were in fact some of her closest followers and they often quickly grasped her message but she always made a point of talking to the men who came to listen. She told her comrades that so many men were wounded and did not know how to deal with it.

Jess realised that they had been out in the countryside for a couple of days and some of those listening had been with her all that time, camping under the stars as she and her friends did. This caused no end of trouble with the Peak District authorities and the local farmers. But she insisted they leave the place untouched, *"leave no trace"* was her motto. Thankfully the weather had been unseasonably good. The Park wardens were even more jittery because of the numbers, but the crowds were so well behaved they turned a blind eye. There were public toilets near by so things were not too bad.

She turned to her comrades and said

'*We need to feed these people they will not be able to find enough to eat round here.*'

They looked at each other and at her,

'*We have hardly any food left either, only some sandwiches.*'

You would have thought they would have remembered the episode at Roche Abbey but they were even more convinced that no one in the crowd had anything to eat this time. Jess again told them to have people sit down in groups and she took the little food they had and she spoke of it as sacred because it was shared and then she began to distribute it. Again it seemed to just keep going, multiplying in people's hands, no one took more than they needed and it just stretched out feeding all present. Did some people get their own food out and share, maybe, but all were fed and there were leftovers!

No Credentials Just Actions

Jess sent people away after they had eaten and she and her friends got back in the vans. They drove back to Maltby to stay with a family and to share in the Catholic Club there. The Catholic Clergy from the fact-finding mission had followed her and took her into a back room, she went with them willingly but they began to interrogate her.

'*You seem to be making some pretty wild claims about yourself, what are your credentials, you have no formal training, can you give us some evidence, some references or can you tell us where you got all these ideas from, can you offer some guarantee that your ministry is valid?*'

Jess put her head in her hands and sighed, '*Why do you all think that degrees and endorsements by some hierarchy makes someone acceptable or not? I have nothing to say to you, no credentials apart from my actions*'.

Forgotten Food and a Missed Point

She walked out and her comrades rushed out after her, they all climbed into the vans and headed for Wickersly.

Because they had left so quickly her friends had forgotten to pack any food, although one of them still had a loaf of bread from the Great Meal they had shared earlier. She talked as they drove,

'Now then friends'

Smiling she looked around the van at them all,

'You need to be really careful about the influence of the those who think they are in charge of Churches or any religion for that matter and even more so about the very powerful who run everything else.

You need to know that they are all part of the same system, though they don't think they are. That system becomes a dragon that needs to be fed.

If you start to buy into their way of doing things it's like getting a computer virus, it starts to eat away at your hard drive till its wiped everything out and your identity has been stolen.

Its like the yeast in beer or bread, if it's off or out of date then it ruins the whole batch, no beer and no bread for the people, beware these so called leaders who ruin it for everyone in the name of progress.'

Her friends started poking each other and giving each other accusatory looks. They thought she was somehow having a go at them for forgetting to bring food.

'Good grief don't you get what I am on about? What does it matter that you forgot the food. How much was left over when we fed those two massive groups of people, in those Great Meals?'

'Loads and loads' they answered her.

'What does that tell you then, how dim are you lot, compare me and the fact finders and what do you get?'

They looked at each other puzzled but did not dare ask any more questions for fear of looking even dimmer.

What Does it Really Mean to See?

They came into Denaby Main and set up shop in the grounds of St Alban's Catholic Church. At this time everywhere they went they would open the backs of the vans and give out whatever had been donated to them, food, clothes, money, and also information about recovery groups, and various forms of help.

Some of the older people who lived in the sheltered accommodation nearby brought an old man on a Zimmer frame who was blind through macular degeneration. She took him away from the crowds onto the playground of the school.

'What's your name?' Jess asked,

'Albert Phelan and I am seventy two years old', the man answered.

Jess took some olive oil out of her pocket and anointed the man's eyes with it. She held her hands over his eyes for some minutes.

'Do you see anything now?' Jess asked.

Albert squinted and then gasped,

'I can see the people outside the church but they look very blurry as if they are in a mist, but its better than it has been for years'.

'Now, lets have another go Albert' Jess said. 'Just because you are old doesn't mean we shouldn't do the best we can for you.'

She put her palms over the man's eyes again, this time for even longer. When she took them away Albert wept.

'I can see everything really clearly.'

'Brilliant Albert, come on I'll take you home, we don't need to make any fuss, we'll get you a paper and you can read the news, not that it will do you much good, these reporters don't know how to raise the heart they just depress the soul, but you are wise enough to be safe I think.'

Albert nodded and they shuffled back to his bungalow. She begged him to keep secret who had helped him.

'Who do you think I am?' Jess returned and packed them into the vans to set off for Harrogate. A major political summit, the G20, was opening, senior world leaders were gathering along with anti globalisation protestors all kept

apart by a huge amount of security, both Police and Secret Service personnel.

Touring some of the towns around the area, Wetherby, Spofforth, and Knaresborough, she attracted a fair amount of attention, she had been featured on the BBC's Look North and ITV's Calendar; raising all kinds of questions about her.

She gathered her closest comrades and helpers, the originals she called them, the first twelve women and men who had gone along with her back in Edlington and they sat down to a barbecue in the park on the edge of Harrogate town centre. After they had eaten, turning to them she asked:

'Who do folk think I am, what do they say I'm about?'

There was an awkward silence and then one by one they offered various opinions.

'Some people think that somehow you are Rumi the Drowner, that his spirit has somehow passed in to you.'

Some of them smiled at the naïveté of this as they had seen them together.

'Others say you are like Ghandi or Martin Luther King or Mother Theresa or some Guru because you offer people a new way of living.'

There were lots of nods and nudges.

Jess looked at each one in turn and then said,

'But I want to know what you all think, who do you think I am?'

Rob gulped and blurted out what had been growing in his mind:

'I think that somehow you are Jesus come back, I have known you since we were kids but now you're not like anyone I have ever met, anyway wouldn't Jesus be ordinary. I reckon you have the real message about how to run the world and that you are here to change everything, somehow . . . .' He trailed off, bright red with embarrassment looking at the rest, daring them to laugh.

But Jess looked extremely serious. She told them to say nothing about what Rob had blurted out, neither confirming what he had said nor denying it. She told them to say nothing of this conversation to anyone, especially not the press. She had often warned them about the media.

In the Lion's Den She went on: *'What I will say is that my version of what makes a leader is very different to the ones not more than half a mile from here with their Secret Services and need for millions and millions of pounds of security.*

One day soon I will walk right into the lion's den, the snake pit they have created and let them bare their teeth and fill me with their venom. I will take everything they have to throw at me until it kills me.

When you see violence and oppression look out, it is never the last word. When this all happens I will show you how the Great Turning is always the last word.'

'Over My Dead Body' When he could grab a moment to drag Jess aside Rob took her to task, saying there was no way he would allow that kind of thing to happen to her, basically saying 'over my dead body!'

Jess noticed that the others were looking in their direction and obviously straining to hear them.

She rounded on Rob: *'Your words and the thoughts behind them are much darker than you think; you won't help me talking like that, with the twisted logic of the system, the way the powers want us to think. Some battles have to be fought and lost, the labour pains of the Great Emergence, that's how this all works and you'd better get your head round it and pretty damn quick.'*

Rob looked crestfallen and slouched off to the others. But Jess called the groups of people sitting on the green to come and gather round her and her comrades. She seemed to be firing on all cylinders after what had just happened.

Let Go of the System *'Look, if you really want the Great Turning you have to change sides, let go of the system in your heads and* in your hearts, don't judge your bodies by the standards of the glossy magazines, in fact don't judge yourselves at all, drop all that, let it die, and wake up to the Great Self that is given to you, so you can live in a new way.

Having more and more stuff doesn't make you secure, avoiding the idea that one day you will die doesn't mean you won't, ignoring the effects of your actions on others including those on the other side of the world doesn't mean they don't have one, and worse you could wake up one day feeling utterly empty, the life you thought you had will be like a bad dream.

Trust me, you can use that emptiness and the nightmares to propel you into the Great Emergence and out of the system, then a new life will be born in you everyday, full of challenges, yes, but also the joy of knowing that you are part of a Great Turning.

I ask you, what use is wealth or fame or power, if you have to live in a cage to protect yourself from everything that is actually worth having. When the media hound your every step and can't wait to pull you into the mud.

If any of you who have really felt the power of the Great Turning and then allowed it to slip through your fingers by climbing the greasy pole and gaining some mirage of control then you are in deep trouble.

If you, and this is even worse, make religion into another place about who's in and who's out, then I promise you, you will be deeply embarrassed when someone like me reminds you about the Great Turning.

Watch out, if you drown out the voice of the Great Emergence, sooner or later you will think it is a threat and eliminate its call wherever you find it. At that time try to remember these words, because if you don't you will be eliminating any chance of a deep fulfilment.

I am really sure of this, there are some of you standing here now that will feel the full force of the Great Turning very soon, even before you die'.

A Light in the Hills She took them on a long trek from Harrogate, the longest hike most of them had ever made. Each night they found local campsites and pitched tents, people heard they were coming and laid on food for them and in return Jess shared with them and looked after all those in need, her friends were now well trained to help her.

Ninth Blog
North Yorkshire,
Ingleborough,
Edlington,
Castleton,
Sheffield
Birmingham
Manchester,
Glasgow,
Newcastle,
March-April
2012

On the fifth day of walking she took Rob, Jeff, and Julie climbing Ingleborough[8] whilst her friends kept the people away so that they could have some time alone.

Jess stood there gazing into the distance and after a while her face began to shine, some inner light suffusing her, then her whole body seemed to glow with a radiance, from nowhere, a number of figures emerged around her in the shimmering light, there were men and woman and they were talking with her.

Rob burst into the gathering and exclaimed excitedly;

---

[8]   The Highest Peak in Yorkshire

'*Lets pitch some tents and get a fire going so that you can all sit down and talk more comfortably*'.

Just at the moment when he and the others were about to head off down the hill to get the things, a cloud, which had been sitting low over the peak, seemed to lower itself over them all and in the misty beauty the light shone hazily and then really began to dazzle them.

Then all of a sudden they heard a voice, seeming to come from the cloud, though they couldn't be certain; it said:

'*Here is one whom I love so deeply, she is filled all through with love and she will show you what real love means*'.

Then the whole show rolled up like a carpet and disappeared leaving them rubbing their eyes and when they looked again they saw just Jess smiling at them, she turned beckoning them to come back down the hill.

The Great Confrontation

As they followed her down the path she told them not to mention what they had witnessed until after she had been through the Great Confrontation. They obeyed her wishes, not even mentioning it to the others, though they often discussed it with each other as the whole event made such a deep impression on them. They kept coming back to the phrase *Great Confrontation* and they could not, for the life of them, figure out what it meant. They did try and get it out of her on the way down by asking:

'*Who were those people you were with?*'

She answered them

'*They were some of those who have gone before me through death, who were willing to stand up for the truth*'.

Julie asked,

'*Why is it so many great people are killed off like that, why don't people take any notice of them?*'

Jess paused to the think and then said,

'It is true that it seems that no one takes any notice of their message apart from the most exploited and excluded and then when they have been killed the world makes a real show of honouring them with museums, huge churches and holidays in their honour.'

She went on,

'But they offer a vision of what the Great Change feels like. Let me tell you I don't expect to be treated any differently from them, I will have to go through a Great Confrontation, it is the way of things, but each time it is faced the Change gathers more momentum. Yes Jesus embodied it all and look at what they did to him, they honour him with buildings and worship but not by Changing.'

A Difficult Diagnosis This perplexed them greatly and all were lost in thought as they headed back towards the others. Coming closer they saw there was a large crowd and in the middle of it were Jess's friends engaged in a heated exchange with the clergy from the Ecumenical Fact Finding Committee, which now also numbered some civil servants as the politicians were beginning to want answers too.

As soon as the crowd caught sight of Jess they came running up, such was her growing status. Many of the national and local press were there and flashes started going off as photographers and interviewers crowded around. She pulled one of her own people aside and asked:

'What on earth is going on, what's all the fuss about?'

A woman in the crowd overheard her and said:

'Look Miss, I'll tell you as it's my fault this kicked off. I brought me son to your friends because he has been unable to speak for years now, he has the most dreadful stammer, can't say a word, just stands there drooling, opening and shutting his gob. He also has fits where he falls down and just lies there grinding his teeth, totally rigid. I heard your friends 'ad the same powers as you so I asked 'em to help 'im but they were useless they couldn't do nothing.'

Jess looked completely exasperated, she even scowled at them all, which was unusual for her, being very placid most of the time.

'What a world we live in' she sighed, *'full of gadgets and technology but absolutely no understanding of what really goes on inside people'*, turning to her comrades she said, *'how much longer is it going to take to get this stuff through to you? Bring the lad over here to me'*

As soon as the young man got close to Jess, photographers from the press and those brought by the fact-finding group started flashing away, sensing something was about to happen. This immediately induced another fit in the boy and he began to writhe about on the floor and foam at the mouth. Jess laid a hand on the Mother's arm to calm her and asked,

'How long has this been going on?'

Sobbing she looked up at her,

'Since 'e were a little lad, his name is Nick by the way. I've taken him to all sorts of clinics and doctors, even worked at two jobs to pay private but nothing's worked. His Dad left me two years ago said I was obsessed with 'im, but I can't abandon the lad to some psychiatric unit.'

The tears ran down her cheeks as she continued *'Every time 'e 'as a bit of respite and I think 'e's getting better, all of a sudden he'll have a whole load of fits and I am frit that one day he will fall under a car or down the stairs, please if you have any 'eart 'elp us.'*

'Any heart?' Jess said, and left the words hanging in the silence for a minute or so. Everyone stood in suspended animation. She looked deep into the woman's eyes and she looked back, sobs wracking her frame.

'If you embrace this, as it is right now' Jess whispered to her, *'anything can be transformed, the question is can you allow for the chance that it might change, so many people define themselves by their problems and not by their soul'*.

'I really do' the woman blurted out throwing her arms around Jess, *'but I'm stuck in t' dark and can't see a way out'*

The photographers were preparing for another barrage and the reporters were getting their notebooks ready; the crowd, she noticed, was growing and many were elbowing each other aside for a better view.

She knelt down beside the young man and laid her hands on his head and chest and closed her eyes, at first the boy thrashed around even more, a flash went off somewhere and Jess opened her eyes and motioned to her comrades to form a circle around them so that no one could see.

She invited the Mother to hold the boy's hands and then she resumed her quiet vigil. The lad's eyes suddenly shot open and he stared terrified at Jess. Jess began to speak to him in voice no one could hear. She then laid her hands on the boy's head and he gave out a piercing scream and went limp. Someone pushed though the cordon and shouted

'He's dead, the witch has killed him!'

Jess told her helpers to reform the circle and lent down to the young man, he opened his eyes and stood up. She brought Mother and Son together and spoke to them:

'You need to talk to him about what happened to him as a child, ask him to tell you about his uncle, I think he is ready to speak of it now. He will need to get some help to deal with it all.'

A look passed across the Mother's face of utter confusion she looked from Jess to her son and back again. Then again she burst into tears and hugged Jess who was also weeping.

The boy pulled at his Mum's arm:

'I couldn't tell you Mum, he made me swear'.

'I am so sorry, I am sorry, I can't believe it, I am so sorry . . . .'

His mother sobbed and sobbed.

Jess made Tim and Eddie and Bounty take them home on the bus and told them that they were all heading back to Edlington and to meet her there. The crowd were dumfounded and parted to let them through, even the press respected the boy and his Mother and left them alone. Though subsequently a newspaper managed to get hold of a transcript of a police interview and published details of the abuse, the uncle was a minor celebrity. The people dispersed back to their homes, buzzing with all that they had seen.

When they were in the vans travelling home Bethany asked her why they had been unable to do anything for the boy.

Jess looked at them seriously and said:

'Some problems require a depth that only comes with long stretches of silent meditation and even fasting. This sharpens your ability to listen to what is really going on inside someone and to know how to help them.'

A Prediction After a few days back in Edlington they set off on another attempt to be alone. They stayed in the Youth Hostel in Castleton hoping not to be noticed as she had many things she wanted to discuss with them. They walked out into the hills and sitting right at the top of Mam Tor gazing out over a mist covered valley she said to them,

'This Woman[9] will be betrayed to the powers that be, politicians, bankers and religious leaders, they will get rid of her but that will not be the end of the story, a few days after she will reappear.'

They were completely confused and did not really understand what she was trying to say to them but they dare not tell her, so they all nodded and tried to look smart.

An Embarrassing Argument A few days later they were back in Sheffield staying at a

---

[9] When she called herself this she always held her hand over her heart.

Buddhist Centre as many at the place were sympathetic to her ideas and liked her to lead the meditations. When they were having breakfast on the first morning of their stay she asked them:

'What were you arguing about in the mini bus yesterday',

They all looked sheepish and said nothing, so she persisted,

'When I came back from paying for the petrol you were having a right set to about something, what was it?'

They were arguing about who had done the most to help people and then moved on to who could do the longest silent sit without fidgeting. Finally they had quarrelled about which of them Jess spent the most time with and thought the most of. They felt very sheepish now that she had asked them, but at the time it had become quite heated. Jess had caught enough to know what was going on so she said to them:

'Whoever wants preferential treatment and recognition should look deep inside themselves and find a place where that stops being important and live from there.

Status and esteem are not things other people can give you, they come from being in touch with the truth. The truth that you already have all you need, that by being here you matter, by existing you are valuable beyond measure.

But if you want to feel really good about your life then don't try to be first, no, seek the place where you can be ordinary and offer the overlooked the valuing you've found inside.'

At that moment a three-year-old girl came wandering in, she was the child of one of the leaders of the Centre. She stood with her big brown eyes looking up at them and smiling. Jess opened her arms and she ran into them and she sat on her lap, eating cornflakes from the box. Jess looked at her comrades and helpers saying:

'If you can make of your soul a welcoming place like this child has, you will be welcomed also, what you hold in your soul is what you will find offered back to you by the world.

That is how the Great Change enters the world, welcome reality as a powerful stranger and it becomes your intimate friend.'

Friends and Enemies

Later that day as they were all sitting in the lounge, she was talking with them when Jeff asked her,

'Miss Jess[10], we saw this woman at the Alternative Medicine Centre down the road advertising herself as a 'Jess Jennings Teacher' and putting on workshops on recovery and healing for addicts and telling people that you had taught her. So we went in and tried to stop her, we took down her posters and confiscated her leaflets. We told her to come and talk to you before she did anything else'.

Jess looked up and said to Jeff and the others:

'You shouldn't have stopped her; if she really is doing good work under my banner then she won't harm our good name or the reputation of the Great Emergence.

If she is rubbish then people will soon work that out for themselves, you know people can usually suss out bullshit pretty quickly. But if she is really doing things my way she is an ally not an enemy.

Not a Franchise!

The Great Change is not a franchise that we can market so as to build an empire, it is a republic and entry is free to all who want it, the ticket price is to know your need and to accept your own brokenness.

---

[10] This is what they had taken to calling her, as they were beginning to have such a deep respect for her that just calling her Jess seemed too informal, it was what they called their teachers at school

Anyone who hears us and even buys a Big Issue is on our side and those deeds increase the pressure for the Great Turning.'

She paused staring shrewdly at them, sensing their confusion,

'On the other hand, if anyone tries to make an empire out of the Great Change it is like trying to build a city in the middle of the ocean, it will sink.

If people build their reputations around it they will find that the empire they create becomes more important than the simplicity of the work.

If they create hierarchies, forcing out the weakest and the misfits then they'll wish they hadn't.

If they put protection of their institutions over the lives of the young and innocent it would be better they were given concrete shoes and thrown into the ocean.

Just look at what has been done by so called religious people throughout history, burning people in the name of God, killing, making war, excluding the weakest and the poorest, slavery, apartheid, believe me it is easy to convince your-self it's all for God when it's really about your empire, church, tribe or nation and nothing drives out the Great Republic more than that.'

Her friends and helpers looked even more confused.

'Let me be really straight about this' she said 'if something really gets in the way of Great Change even if it is something you think you cannot live without, like your position in society, your reputation, your relationships, then let them go, better to come through into the new world without them than end up stuck in a dead world with your ego fully intact.

Believe me no one escapes the fires of change, but if you go through them willingly they can only do you good. Once on the other side you can lead others through, they will trust you and there will be harmony rather than the endless power games that cause hell on earth.'

A Major Tour   From Sheffield Jess took them on a trip to major cities like Birmingham and Manchester, Glasgow and Newcastle. Wherever she went she gathered crowds of people in Church Halls or Community Centres. In some places municipal halls and pubs were opened to her, as those that ran them thought it might be good for business or their reputation to be associated with her events.

However she never allowed them to affiliate her events with any advertising nor would she endorse any products. If they insisted she refused to share and moved on. When the crowds formed she always engaged fully with them and held them in rapt attention.

Deeper Scrutiny A Home Office Commission comprising leading ecclesiastical bureaucrats

Tenth Blog
Birmingham
Leicester
Forest
Services
April
2012

had replaced the fact-finding mission. Alongside them were a number of senior civil servants who wanted to see if there was anything that implied criticism of the Government or conversely whether she could be used to support their agenda. The Roman Catholic Church had withdrawn from the commission and the Vatican had appointed a team to investigate her, as she was often welcomed into Catholic Churches and buildings and they wanted to scrutinise what she was saying, suspecting it did not fit with Catholic teachings. Some powerful media figures were also dispatching journalists to try and dig up information about her and check her out.

True Union One day, in Birmingham a senior Roman Catholic cleric, Monsignor Smart was in the crowd and he stopped Jess mid sentence,

'Should divorce be allowed, in your opinion?'
She knew he was trying to catch her out.
Quick as a flash she answered,
'What does your Church say?
'No, it isn't allowed, Jesus said what God joins together no man should separate'.
'And the State, what does the law say?'
'Well the state says yes if you go through the legal processes it lays down, but that's not divine law'.
'So' Jess went on 'the Roman Catholic Church says no, the Church of England says, in some circumstances and the state says yes. And you want me to make a great pronouncement, and then I suppose you will follow up with another of your litmus tests like Gay marriage?
Jesus told you what he thought and you have turned that teaching into a way of keeping hurt and broken people just that, hurt and broken, denying them what you would never deny yourselves, yes you know what I am talking about—Holy Communion.
What I will say is this; the sacred bond made between two lovers can last a lifetime and makes them a shelter for children, friends and the needy. They create this and it becomes a beacon of the Great Welcome and can only be judged by its fruit not some outward ceremony. Believe me, Gay or Straight the love is the same.
And if you think you know where it does or doesn't happen you are much wiser than I am. But if you want to promote the power and force of love in the world then support it wherever you find it and don't force people to go through your own version of hell when they make a mistake and are hurt and wounded in the process.
For the sake of the little ones involved whose lives could be forever blighted by their parents' mistakes, look to help them and don't create more problems than their slight shoulders can bear'.
This answer caused huge consternation among the authorities but the people applauded and asked her to tell them more.

When they were staying in an Afro-Caribbean community centre, she told her friends and the people at the centre;

'Don't think I am saying its okay to sleep around, be unfaithful to your partner and just go from one relationship to another. No, I am saying that there is a sacred sharing that goes on when you make love to someone, you create a mirror for the other to see their deepest soul in and to see in your eyes they are loved and loveable just because they exist.

This will lead them to a deep understanding of their place in this world, an appreciation they can pass on to others especially their children. If you mess about with that then you cause havoc in a person's soul and wound them so deeply that, if they do not seek healing, they will pass on those wounds to others.'

The Trouble with the Kids

There was a commotion at the door as the Mothers and Toddlers group tried to get in and bring the kids to Jess so she could talk to the Mums and meet the children. Jess's comrades were telling them not to disturb her as she was sharing, but when Jess figured out what was going on she spoke sternly to her helpers,

'Now then, hang on a minute, let them come in; kids are not an interruption they are what matters. The Great Change is always about young hearts. It is this kind of innocence that makes it happen. A willingness to see things the way they do is the Great Welcome, and if you harm that innocence in yourself or in these little ones you are crippling the Great Turning.'

Then she drew around herself a little crowd of women, babies and toddlers. She spoke with them, telling stories and cuddling the children. One or two were suffering from ailments and she helped to make them better.

Well Heeled and Disappointed

As they were leaving the Centre a young man ran

down the street towards them and greeted Jess as if she were royalty and asked her to sit down and talk. He was very well spoken and confident for a man in his twenties. Though he was wearing jeans, they were Armani and his pink shirt was Ralph Lauren and his blazer was hand made in Saville Row. He had been educated at Ampleforth Catholic public school; he was a city trader and had driven up from London in his Porsche.

He addressed Jess,

'Miss, what do I need to do in order to be truly happy and to be part of the Great Emergence you have been talking about?'

Jess said;

'Why call me Miss, save your politeness for those you want to impress, Jess will do. If you want to be happy then live a good life, don't lie or cheat, look after your family, give to charity, and serve your community'.

He looked crestfallen and replied,

'I do all that, I try to be honest in my dealings, my family are very important to me, I spend time with them, I am on the board of a local drugs charity and arranged a royal visit to its centre last year. I recently became chair of a London pro-life charity and we organise charity balls for the rich and famous to raise money for the pregnancy advisory clinic it runs. I am running the New York Marathon for the restoration of the roof at Westminster Cathedral in a month's time. I know the Cardinal personally and advise him on the City and how the Church can invest its money wisely'.

Jess looked the young man square in the eye and was obviously genuinely impressed by him, she could see that this was a good-hearted young man, well heeled and very earnest.

'Okay, if you really want to go for the Great Change then sell all the things you have and give the money anonymously to Oxfam and come and join us on the road.'

The young man looked at Jess for a long time and his face became ashen and he began to shake his head, he had many possessions, a flat in Knightsbridge, his car, all his investments, works of art and so much more. He shook Jess's hand and tried to give her a cheque for the work. Jess refused it saying

'We want you not your money'.

The man left them and Jess watched him go regret stamped all over her face.

Then Jess looked around at all her friends and the people from the centre and said,

'It is so difficult when you have all kinds of possessions because they begin to possess you. It is easier for an articulated lorry to drive down the shaft at Yorkshire Main Colliery than it is for an affluent and well connected person to accept the Great Change.'

Not In Spite of Madness, Because Of It!

All those around her were utterly astonished by this, Bounty exclaimed.

'Who has any chance then, there are loads of rich people, go to London or the posh bits of any city and you will find shed-loads like him'.

'I know it looks impossible' Jess answered *'the world seems hell bent on committing suicide, not just individuals. It is even worse when companies or countries agree to the lie that money is more important than people.*

I just heard they invented grain that has a suicide gene and once it has produced a crop it kills itself and the seeds from the harvest are sterile.

What kind of minds would tamper with biology like that?

But this is not the end of the story if we trust the deepest energy of the universe, that it is emerging even out of this madness then it starts to look possible, the Great Change is happening not despite our madness but because of it.'

Rob, looked confused and tried another tack, *'Look Miss, we have made a massive commitment to go on the*

*road with you. We have left all sorts of stuff behind and we
have no idea where this is all leading, we just trust you.'*

Jess smiled at him and then looked at them all.

*'The Great Change turns everything upside down.
Anyone who leaves behind the safe harbour of their
security, what many call being sensible, and seeks to make
a better and fairer world will be repaid by seeing that world
become more real every day, what you yearn for is what you
become.*

*And on top of that they will be open to more life than
they know what to do with and this will carry them through
the doors of death into an even greater mystery.*

*The Great Emergence means a total reversal of
priorities, many that think they are top of the league will
find themselves relegated and right down at the bottom and
that could be their salvation.'*

Heading for the Smoke It was at this time she told them
they were going down to London
for Easter, until then Birmingham
was the furthest south they had ventured.

She had arranged to stay just on the edge of the city
and they were all travelling down by various methods to get
to a Jewish Cultural Centre that had invited her to talk to
them.

In one of her recent sharings she had highlighted the
way in which certain groups were scapegoated and the need
for reconciliation and forgiveness. One or two members of
the Centre had been sent to discover what she was about,
to see if she were in any way anti-Semitic, in fact they had
been very touched by her words and actions and asked her
to come and talk about the Palestinian problem.

Jess and her comrades set off in their vans ahead of
the little convoy of vehicles that had been gathered for the
trip, the group had grown significantly. Her closest friends
were bemused and a little scared to be going to London and
fearful of what might happen there. So she began to go over
what they should expect.

'We are going to London and I am going to be arrested by the authorities, I will disappear and they will have me tortured and executed in secret, and after a few days I will reappear again.'

Jeff and Julie, like the rest, could *To Control or to Serve* not get their heads around this and acted like she never said it. They were aware from some of her preparations that there were to be a series of actions and that Jess's idea of the Great Change was to be proclaimed in a new and stronger way.

So they focussed on that, asking her;

'Miss, we want you to do something for us.'

She answered; *'Tell me, I will see what I can do'*.

'When we take power in London can we be your right hand people and run the show, we are getting good at this now and can make sure everything is handled properly.'

She gave a wry smile and looked at them hard and said,

'You've no idea have you. What you are asking is to be with me as I go through a baptism of fire, as I face the darkness that is at the heart of the city and the heart of the system, can you cope with that, can you?'

They looked at each other and shrugged,

'Why not, how hard can it be?' Jeff said.

'We have been with you from the start Miss, we can handle the pressure and we will get things organised', Julie added.

'Okay, okay you will be with me when I have to go through the belly of this beast, as for being in charge, well the Great Change will be responsible for who serves it, so you will have to wait and see.'

When the others realised what was being discussed they were indignant feeling that somehow Jeff and Julie had stolen a march on them. They started complaining and blaming the pair.

It was beginning to get pretty heated as things do on the road. So she silenced them addressing the whole group.

'Look, you know in the business world and in politics, even in the Churches, that leadership is seen as a privilege, travelling first class, eating in the best places. This changes their view of the world and they lose touch with the people they are supposed to be leading.

The power very quickly becomes more important than the ability it gives them to change things, hanging on to it becomes the priority.

Please do not let it be that way with you.

Whoever is looking for true greatness should look for the best ways to serve. The first place is not to be confused with the top place, becoming fully aware of your calling means finding the gift inside you that will serve the most people and finding ways to make that gift a reality.

Look at me, I am just a woman from Edlington and I am here to throw myself under the wheels of the Great Change, to be the oil that smoothes its progress, even to give my life itself to make it happen.'

Bad Language They stopped at Leicester Forest services and after they had eaten and used the facilities they were coming out through the doors when a man who regularly tried to beg around the site and was even more regularly ejected, started to shove through the crowd that had formed around Jess.

He had suffered from Tourette's syndrome since he was a child and could not help the ticks and outbursts of swearing and profanity that exploded from him, sometimes these even led to physical violence and spitting.

He pleaded with Jess to help him, shouting and flinching, the crowd parted around him and many were telling him to be quiet, but that just made his ticks worse and he pleaded all the more vocally. Jess stopped dead and ordered them to bring him over and they said to him *'Hey you're in luck, she wants to see you'*.

Jess took the man over to the van and sent everyone away expect her closest friends and asked the man;

'What do you think I can do for you'?

The man's reply was punctuated with many ticks and outbursts; the gist of his request was this;

'Since I was a kid I have been plagued by this Tourette's, it is like another person acting through me, I have hardly any friends, my family have slowly abandoned me and I feel so lonely. I have often hit the people I love and I cannot even sit in the front of a car for fear I will grab the wheel and crash the car. I know you probably can't cure me but I just need some relief, one tick free day would be heaven.'

Jess was obviously very moved by the man, she asked him to sit in the van and sent everyone away. She spent over an hour with him and when they emerged the man was completely calm. Jess was telling him,

'Remember what we have done together, that moment when you could talk to the part of yourself that is angry and isolated and wants to be heard. I cannot promise you are cured but keep talking to him, he is a part of you he is lost and he wants to come back in.'

The tears were streaming down the man's face and he hugged Jess.

'I want to stay with you and help you' He said.

'Then stay' Jess offered *'we won't judge you, but we are going into a lions den in London, so be warned it could be really tough'*.

'Tough's fine by me, I have done tough all my life'.

So he joined them and he became a very close friend to Jess, ticks and all.

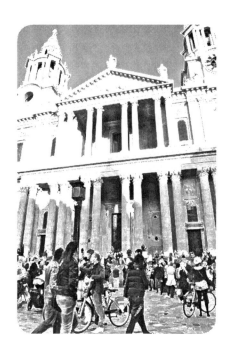

Bikes for Change
As they were approaching London the plans Jess had been forming for some weeks came to very swift fruition. She gave her talk on Scapegoating at the Cultural Centre and was well received. Some of the press reported that she was a Palestinian agitator, though others said she was considering embracing Judaism.

The next day she set in motion the opening phases of her plan. She had decided to ride into London on a pushbike from the end of the M1 motorway at the Brent Cross Shopping Centre right into the centre, finishing up with a rally in Trafalgar Square.

She called it the *Ride for Change*, a website had been set up and the word was spreading rapidly. The President of the USA was arriving that day for a state visit and was to be taken from Downing Street to Buckingham Palace, Jess aimed to time her entry into central London to coincide with that journey.

The following morning she had arranged to gather in the car parks and waste ground around the Brent Cross Shopping Centre. Her comrades expected a few hundred people, they were astonished to see thousands and thousands had gathered, all with their bikes, men, women and a large number of children. The police were completely taken by surprise and were trying to bar their entrance to the end of motorway but sheer weight of numbers overwhelmed them, people just poured onto the road.

So many were there that, gradually the traffic had to just slow down and finally came to a standstill. Jess at the front of the column was using a megaphone to tell the people how their action was part of the Great Emergence and that change came when people put their hearts and souls into action, she called it soul-force and talked of Ghandi and Martin Luther King. She then started to teach them chants about the Great Turning and the sound of their voices became like a tidal wave of sound converging on central London.

By the time they were getting near to the centre the police were ahead of them, out-riders and cars, stopping the traffic and trying to manage the chaos. The Presidents motorcade in which he and the Prime Minister were riding had to be halted and was forced to wait for three quarters an hour, thus making them late for the Queen.

When Jess finally arrived in Trafalgar Square they lifted her onto the empty plinth and through her megaphone she addressed the crowds about the Great Change. The crowds cheered and applauded constantly calling for more. They chanted the chants she had taught them over and over again. Then she led them in a twenty-minute silent meditation. The sight of thousands of people, standing, sitting, eyes closed in rapt attention was striking and even drew in many tourists into what she called the Great Silence. It was something she constantly practised with those who listened to her. She told them that the Great Silence was a key to the Great Emergence and the soil in which the Great Turning would grow.

After the silence Jess, with her comrades and helpers walked down to Westminster Abbey, she tried to enter in order to meditate privately but she realised that she and her friends would have to pay an entrance fee, as they were not attending a service. She turned on her heels seething. She and her friends managed to get away from the crowds and took the tube to East London where they were the guests of the Brick Lane Mosque, who wanted to hear her speak and to talk about her ideas on scapegoating. They gave her an hour on her own to meditate before asking her to share with them.

The media were agog, not for a long time had anyone sparked such a spontaneous reaction from so many ordinary people. The evening news broadcasts were headlined by footage of Jess leading her bike ride down onto the M1 and people chanting in Trafalgar Square. The story knocked all the sound bites of the President and the Prime Minister off the top of the News as the media preferred to show constant rolling footage of them looking grouchily on as they were caught in the traffic jam.

The Locked Church—Part One The next day as she was on her way to get the tube back into central London she noticed a large church set back off the road, she decided to go in and meditate. The church was locked; every door they tried was shut and bolted. She was furious, and shouted at the great double doors of the building;

'You had a chance to open your doors and let those in need enter and find peace, now you will never be opened again'.

Her friends looked at each other bemused and shrugged, but they remembered what she had said.

Crashing the System They came out of the tube station and walked towards St Paul's Cathedral. Her arrival had been expected as her followers had sent out emails and texts telling everyone who would listen to gather on the steps of St Paul's at eleven and await Jess's instructions. It had also been posted on a Great Turning Website that some of them had set up.

There was a very large crowd spilling onto the roads all around and holding up the traffic. Her followers had rigged up a portable PA and she began to talk to the crowd about the system that surrounded them.

She pointed at the skyscrapers that housed the stock market and the major banks and she spoke of how the system was strangling the life out of the people and that it functioned by creating billions of losers and hundreds of winners.

She then went on to the politicians and told the crowd that they too had failed to bring about the Great Change (or even a small change), that they had settled for things as they were and had no vision of things as they could be.

She then pointed at all the steeples around and the great dome of the cathedral. She wept as she said that the Churches had failed even more so because they had been closest to the vision of the Great Turning and not accepted it, that Church Leaders had been infected with the same disease as the Bankers and the Politicians, that of protecting themselves and their positions rather than caring for the weakest and least.

She then proclaimed a new republic, the Republic of Hope.

'The republic of Hope was inaugurated thousands of years ago and I am here to re-establish its credentials.

The universe is a place of beauty and wonder and our planet sits in the scintilla of possibilities and in that narrow band of fortune she offers life to all who live on her.

The paradise that is on offer has been hijacked by greed, an unquenchable thirst for prestige, power and possessions has turned Eden into Hades for all but the very rich and they even have to barricade themselves in for fear that they will lose what they think they have.

*Today I want you all to reboot the system, to show
how we could reprogramme the life of this planet and find
the lost Garden of Eden.'*

The Republic of Hope
She proceeded to send her friends among the crowd and start giving out the call to Action for Change; the signal for a mass campaign of emailing, texting, tweeting and posting instructions to all those who followed her online. What followed was extraordinary.

Thousands of ordinary people started opening bank accounts with £10 deposits and then closing them again, both in branches and online. They started buying individual shares and then selling them again. If they made a profit they would give it to charity. They went into banks and bureau de change and exchanged small amounts into foreign currency and then into other outlets to change it back into sterling. The whole financial system became massively clogged up and that in turn caused worries on the stock market.

Coupled with this thousands more ordinary people began to send emails to the CEOs and leaders of major companies demanding they clean up their practices, this would have been easy to ignore if they had not also started picketing city centre shops and the great shopping malls persuading people that these were to be three *zero shopping days* and for that time they were invited to refrain from shopping, except for essentials and thereby to do the planet a favour. This request was emailed to people too so that there was a massive slump in online purchasing.

On top of that others entered the head offices of multinational corporations and finance houses, major banks and Internet companies, demanding meetings with the top management and asking them to account for their decisions about tax and corporate responsibility and also their salaries.

Many of these *Agents for Change* (as they called themselves) were accompanied by news cameras and reporters; it was impossible for the security guards to eject them, especially as many of them were mothers and toddlers or disabled people.

A great call was made for new homes, *Homes for Change*. Somehow Jess had brought together all the leading housing charities and house builders and they lobbied the banks to lend them money to build desperately needed houses or refurbish brown field sites, thus providing jobs and homes.

The final act of the drama around the banks was the setting up of the great Perspex box in front of the bank of England. A huge clear plastic box around ten feet square had been made with a letterbox sized opening in the side. Ordinary people were asked to donate ten percent of their salaries for that week, and the request was posted on the Internet asking the city executives to match this generosity. For many this was a small amount, but for a person earning upwards of one hundred thousand pounds a year it was not insignificant.

The money was to go towards one off grants to help those made unemployed by the crash establish new cooperatives and kick-start their lives and the economy. A whole new trust was set up by a group of enlightened community and business leaders to administer this. By the end of the three days of action there were twelve boxes full of cash and numerous cheques made out by highly paid executives who were either shamed into the gesture or genuinely wanted to make reparation. Millions of pounds were donated, either in the person or online in virtual boxes.

Don't Read All About It The media companies themselves were not immune from the *Agents'* attentions. An online campaign was launched to have a three-day moratorium on buying newspapers and watching or listening to any TV or Radio, and an email campaign to editors was launched asking for a new approach. Some of the requests were that they agree never to pay for a story again; that they become cooperatives owned by any member of the public who wanted to invest and also for their staff to have a share in the business, in the style of John Lewis; and finally that the great press and business monopolies across the board be broken up and transferred to cooperative ownership. It became very clear to the powers that be in the media that somehow, and without their help, her message had become far more widespread than they had imagined. Word of mouth had become her primary medium through hundreds of small gatherings.

Shock Waves and After Shocks

By the end of the first day the FTSE 100 had dropped by twenty percent and financial commentators were talking of the London Contagion as it began to spread to other countries. Throughout the day, as each country woke up to the news, actions spread and the Dow Jones suffered similar losses, as did markets across the world.

The campaigns were written off by *the powers that be* as a blip and they sent out press releases saying that things would return to normal soon. Of course many never saw them because of the press boycott. But secretly it was reported that the markets were deeply rattled by what had happened. The organic nature of the action made it uncontrollable and that created uncertainty and therefore widespread panic on trading floors and in investment houses.

The Politics of Silence

Of the thousands in the crowd outside St Paul's many embarked on a march to parliament and a mass lobby of MPs. They had one simple request; that the politicians engage in a twenty-four-minute silence in the chamber as an act of solidarity with all those across the world who have suffered in the financial crisis.

They asked that each MP stand in silence and in so doing make a vow to find a way to change the system so it would never happen again. The time set for this was three pm. Amazingly this too spread virally across the world, even members of both houses in the USA held their own twenty-four-minutes silence, though many had no idea that the whole thing had originated from the steps of St Paul's and an unemployed Hair Dresser from Edlington.

Faith enough to stop shooting Another initiative that stemmed from this epicentre was the 24-hour ceasefire. A whole website had been dedicated to this by some of the *agents for change*. It was to take place on the second day of Jess's three days of action.

All kinds of websites picked it up, along with bloggers who very quickly started posting comments. Within hours it was one of the major headlines on Al Jazeera, as the news travelled all across the Middle East and further into Afghanistan and beyond.

It called upon all those who wanted to honour God, to prove their faith by laying down their weapons and to fast during the hours of daylight, the Muslims began to call it a day like Ramadan in honour of the Prophet.

Surprisingly each religious group or faction somehow viewed this as a way of proving their religion was authentic. The Israeli's called it a day of special atonement and many Hindus celebrated the cease-fire as the Diwali of Diwalis, a day for good to triumph over evil.

Even more astonishing was the fact that people of all faiths and those with none sensed this was their chance to shine. Even gangs in Juarez, Mexico laid down their weapons for the day. What was extraordinary was that this was not an initiative that came from the leaders; in fact many of the leaders ordered the fighting to continue. No, this came from the rank and file, ordinary soldiers and fighters.

In the weeks after Jess's days of action, pictures were shown across the world of British soldiers in Afghanistan flying kites with young children right in the middle of no man's land, where the day before they had been ambushed by the Taliban. In Jerusalem the checkpoints were left unmanned and there was an amazing photograph of a Palestinian women breaking the fast at sunset and giving bread to an Israeli guard and both were laughing! All of this spread virally through individuals, not at the behest of any media empire.

Days of Amnesty   The last action to emerge that day was proclaimed directly by Jess to the throng gathered outside the great church, it was one of great simplicity though it deeply unnerved the Churches and their leaders.

The message went out that the next three days were to be *Three Days of Amnesty*. Anyone who had hurt or damaged another person could contact them and seek to make amends; if that individual was in agreement they were to meet in a sacred place, Church, Mosque, Synagogue, Gurdwara or Temple, stone circle or even an ancient pagan shrine.

Once there they could talk or do whatever was necessary to make recompense to the other. The injured party had to agree to come and there was to be no coercion. This created an explosion of disruption in many religious buildings, especially Churches; priests and leaders were forced to open their buildings for seventy two hours or risk looking out of step with such a good cause.

Services were overrun with people returning stolen goods, weeping in each other's arms and generally rebuilding shattered relationships. Many regular worshippers were surprisingly put out to find their buildings so full and some even locked the amnesty seekers out during worship! Unfortunately more and more of the regular congregations saw this as evidence of a cult surrounding Jess and therefore rejected it out of hand.

People travelled from all over the country to meet each other, family members who had not spoken for years reconnected and what was so effective was that there are sacred places in most towns and villages. This amnesty movement also spread across Europe, the USA, and beyond.

Silence for Change   To the surprise of the Police it also became a time to hand over illegal weapons, drugs, pornography and other illicit material. Churches and other places of worship were suddenly inundated with contraband.

Over those three days Jess and her friends camped out on the steps of the great Church and St Paul's became a hub for all these activities. Hundreds of homeless people slept out with those who followed *Jess's Way* as many began to name it.

People dubbed the steps 'Sleeping Bag Central' as the whole area became a city of cardboard and rough sleepers. The Police seemed powerless to move them on, as the actions were so popular.

As the people involved in *Jess's Way* boycotted official media, all kinds of Blogs and Websites sprang up, videos were posted and various creative ways of networking and sharing emerged. People gathered in public spaces, pubs, clubs, squares and plazas to tell stories and share experiences regarding events. In a podcast Jess called it the Great Democratisation. She explained that the Great Turning was most present when no one group or individual was in control, then all the people would find a voice and a place.

She also launched the 'Silence for Change' *Jess's Way* initiative. This involved her closest comrades recording a series of You Tube videos on the theme of how to find silence in everyday life. Turning off the car radio and driving quietly, rising twenty minutes earlier and sitting in silence with a cup of tea, having silent times together, turning off the TV and sitting for ten minutes. Campaigns were launched to have music turned off in public places and have silent zones in offices. One of the most popular campaigns was the 'Stop the Noise and Start to Live' movement. They advocated fasting from electronic communication for parts of the day and getting outside into nature. 'Listeners for Change' was another aspect of this work. Jess's comrades had learnt the value of sitting and listening to people and allowing them to air their deepest fears. They began to train others in this simple human gift. At night one could see small groups by torchlight on the steps of the old church practising this revolutionary listening. Many other initiatives sprang from this that were so small so as to not be noticed or reported but were still very effective.

A New Use for an Old Church St Paul's became a nerve centre for *The Days of Amnesty* with high profile events happening seemingly in a spontaneous fashion.

A major bank that had always sought to act ethically invited people with bad credit ratings to come so that the Bank could deal with their debts and make them part of a new movement called Amnesty Banking.

This entailed having your debts to loan sharks and disreputable companies paid in return for a commitment to take a seed bed of seven thousand pounds to use to get back into work and onto an even keel.

They agreed to continue to bank with the ethical bank and to build cooperative movements that would change the way in which people traded. To show how this could be done booths were set up all round St Paul's, they were incredibly popular and people traded services and expertise instead of cash.

The authorities in the Cathedral were horrified as services were disrupted not to mention all the individual amnesty meetings going on. They claimed to be in favour of the work; yet one senior cleric preached a sermon saying that people seemed to have forgotten this was the house of God not a market place.

In a speech to end *The Days of Amnesty* Jess reminded the Church Authorities that doing good for the broken and indebted was, in her eyes the best worship that could be offered and asked them to count how many extra people had been through the doors of the churches compared with their normal attendances. An increase replicated all over the country and beyond, and not just in Churches; Mosques and Temples, Synagogues and Shrines reported the same. She pointed out the way in which people were devising their own ceremonies of change and reconciliation. All kinds of symbols were used, water, fire, earth and light. Wasn't that what religion was for she asked them, to bind people together again?

'You have lost your way, you want the Republic of Love to fit into your boxes so you can dispense it in a way that suits your view of the world. You fight endless battles about who is acceptable, gay or straight, male or female, right or wrong. Love is not interested in that; love doesn't have a box, just a world created with the message **to be shared** *written through every atom. Some of you want to live in it but as long as you live in your boxes you won't see it.'*

Authority in Question

This unnerved many of the Church Leaders; they felt their authority was being undermined. They held a secret summit, details of which were only leaked later, at which the Archbishops of Canterbury and York and the Catholic Cardinal of Westminster, along with many other denominational leaders were in attendance.

They were stunned by what had happened and reported that the Government was seriously angered by Jess and her people and were asking the Church leadership what they were going to do about this anarchic rabble carrying on under its very roofs, apparently with its tacit approval. The Prime Minister made it very clear he expected action.

Though they called them a rabble, what had shocked all them all was the viral nature of the change and how it appeared to be coordinated. As Jess had intended the three days of action represented a microcosm of what might be possible if people woke up to the message of the Great Change. The powers that be sensed that their very ability to rule was being challenged at its core.

The Locked Church—Part Two

Jess returned to East London, the elders of the mosque took them out for a meal in

Bangla Town, a Bangladeshi cultural centre in the Brick Lane area after which they were farmed out to stay with families across Tower Hamlets. The next day as they were preparing to go back into the Cathedral they noticed that the Church she had spoken of had been demolished, it was now a pile of rubble.

Rob was shocked, *'Look the Church you spoke to yesterday, its gone, just like you said'.*

Jess looked at the rubble and then at her friends.

'This Great Emergence, this Great Turning, if you really go for it then you will find a lever and a place to stand that will overturn the largest of obstacles.

You can take the things of the past like this Church and recycle them into something of great value to those in need. You could recycle the whole of Canary Wharf and make it a place for people and not money, you can take a wasteland and make it into a flowering garden.

But the place to stand is not one of opposition and anger; just watch those MPs on either side of the house; Labour and Conservative in the end they become what they hate! No, stand on the ground of what you are for, what you yearn to see come into reality. Speak to that yearning in those who oppose you. Release them from your judgement and then there is a chance of real change. The Great Energy flows most freely where there is forgiveness and release'.

Show us your Credentials They arrived back in central London and St Paul's where the work carried on apace. A delegation sent by the secret summit of Church Leaders asked to have a meeting with her. They invited her and her helpers to come to the Church of England Head Offices at Great Smith Street. They filed into a room with a large boardroom table but she refused to sit at the table asking that they go to a room without tables and sit in a circle. They had agendas printed, and a report from the Home Secretary's advisors full of questions about the action Jess was unleashing.

She again refused their way of doing business and *said 'Let's do it this way; you get to ask me a question then I ask you one and so on and we will see if we can't touch the truth that way.'*

They seemed wrong-footed by this but after some private discussion they looked satisfied that they had a question to catch her out.

'Can you show us your credentials for all of this you are doing, who gave you the authority to engage in such actions? As far as we know you don't even have proper Hairdressing qualifications let alone any kind of degree or professional training.'

Jess did not miss a beat she looked them straight in the eye and said *'Okay, here's my question, where do you and your Churches get your authority from?'*

They were, again, off balance, they went into a little huddle ignoring Jess as she sat calmly opposite them.

One of them said *'If we say it comes from the Bible the Catholics will be upset, if we say from the Bishops and the Pope then the evangelicals will disagree'*, they therefore said,

'We are not prepared to discuss our authority, it is you who should answer our questions that is the way this works, we ask—you answer'.

She stood up and shook all their hands, *'If you can't tell me where you get your mandate then you won't have a chance of understanding mine, may the Great Emergence illuminate your hearts, goodbye'*.

Having shaken their hands and followed by her friends she left the offices. The delegation were dumfounded, but once they had gathered their wits and their papers they followed her out into the street as they wanted to see what was going to happen next. When she saw that they were right behind she turned to them and said,

Missing the Point

Twelfth Blog London April 2012

'*Okay if you are all still so curious then come with me I want to show you something.*'

She took them to Westminster Cathedral and walked up the aisle, she went and sat down next to an old lady, surrounded by carrier bags, with broken down shoes and a grubby raincoat. She put her arm around her shoulder and sat with her for a good ten minutes. She then stood, stared around at the grandeur of the building and walked towards the door.

'*What do you think you just witnessed?*'

They were confused, '*We didn't witness anything*' they said '*you just went in and then came out again, you never said a word*'.

'*How can you be so blind?*' she admonished them.

The Great Oak and the Great Acorn

She took them to a Coffee Shop and sat them down.

'I want to tell you a story' she said, so they all pulled out notebooks and laptops hoping that what she said would incriminate herself.

'There was once a great oak, a legendary tree yet for many, many years it produced no acorns.

It was prophesied that when an acorn finally grew it would be the most powerful and magical thing the world had ever seen.

People built a great fence around the tree and had ceremonies to worship the tree.

A whole class of clerics emerged dedicated to perpetuating the worship of the tree.

Kings would dedicate their victories in battle to the acorn that was to come.

The Great High Keeper of the Tree was more important than almost anyone else in the entire world.

One day a young rebel came who saw things differently and he managed to climb the tree and found in the topmost branches an acorn.

The Great High Keeper of the Tree and all functionaries of the Tree Precinct and those who lived around the tree, (deriving huge profits from the pilgrims), were furious.

As the young man plucked the acorn unseen by any of them, they threw ropes around the branch he was on and it fell with a great crash.

The young man was killed and his friends took his body away, only to find the acorn still in his hand.

When they told the people some believed and some refused saying it was a lie and a sacrilege to the Great Tree and its High Keeper.

Those who had the acorn kept it and placed it in a mountain shrine and gradually the new Religion of the Acorn grew up.

Those original friends became known as the Custodians of the Acorn and those to whom they passed the role of Custodian too became venerated and powerful and of course, in time very wealthy.

The acorn gradually shrivelled and lost its vitality.

Many years later a woman came and told them she had a message from the Great Mother of both Tree and Acorn.

The Acorn was for planting, she said, so that many trees would grow and all people would find shelter and the great oxygen of life the trees would provide would change the world.

Even now she said, the acorn, if planted would fruit.

Both the Keepers of the Tree and the Custodians of the Acorn alike were incensed and they joined forces saying if we do not get rid of her then we will lose our power so they plotted and plotted and finally had her killed.

What do you think the people of the world will feel about the Keepers and Custodians?' she asked

'Don't you think that the majority of them will think that all their ceremonies and power games were a waste of time or worse a distraction from the truth. And even more terrible all those poor people those who could have benefited from the planting will have been betrayed and will never trust them again.

Have you heard the cliché 'hidden in plain sight', well that is the truth about you people, it is staring you in the face and you avoid it at all costs.'

They were enraged by this story, as they knew it was aimed at them. They stormed out of the coffee shop and went back to the Church Leaders seething with anger and a resolve to do something about her.

This is the Republic of Hope The following day, being the final day of action found her again at St Paul's working with the teams who were monitoring the demonstrations and actions aimed at the financial institutions. She kept telling them to search for *Agents of Change* who could inspire the people and could learn how to take action that was both symbolic and effective. She recorded Internet broadcasts to help train them. She kept insisting this is bigger than one woman; it had to be beyond the charisma or power of any one leader, this is the Republic of Hope she told anyone who would listen.

A Matter of Benefit Number Ten, the Prime Minister's office sent a group of advisers to cross examine and catch her out. Because she refused to give interviews it was hard to get friendly media outlets to fire questions at her that might trip her up. During one of her sessions on the steps of the Cathedral one of them interrupted and said,

'*We know you don't do press interviews. We also know that you are indifferent to public opinion and are not frightened to be completely open about many matters, we wanted to know this—should people cheat the benefit system or should they be reported and locked up?*'

Jess turned to the group of suited and slick men answering,

'*See that guy over there?*' she pointed to a young man sitting in a recovery circle (these were all over the cathedral—places where people could share and seek recovery from their addictions), '*he has just lost his job in a hotel, washing up, how much is he entitled to if he signs on?*'

They all muttered among themselves and then the original questioner answered:

'*We would need to know his exact details, how much he earned whether he has savings; it is very complex.*'

'*Would it be over one hundred and fifty pounds a week?*' she enquired.

'*God. No!*' he replied, shocked.

'*Let me ask you another question then, what was your expenses claim for last week?*'

The man was looking distinctly uncomfortable,

'*It's none of your business, what's that got to do with benefit cheats anyway, answer the question.*'

'*I would bet that it was more than a hundred pounds maybe more than a hundred and fifty, so answer me this, what is the difference between a benefit cheat and an* advisor who pays a tax accountant to make sure he avoids as much tax as possible?'

'*He is on the right side of the law*' the man leapt up from his seat papers flying everywhere.

'*Because the law is made by people like you and it is there to serve you, those who have next to nothing are easy targets. You all should be ashamed of yourselves; you should be serving justice not ambition. Remember this, you cannot make justice serve your self-interest and still turn to it when you need it. Find the courage to live for a week on benefits and then answer your own question!*'

The crowd burst into spontaneous applause and the man sat down red faced and angry.

Reason and Rationality An impromptu question and answer session developed, a humanist guy stood up and asked her,

'*Don't you think that religions are the cause of much of the evil in the world and that the best thing you could do is encourage people to finally abandon them for a life of reason and rationality?*'

She pondered for a moment and then replied:

'*You want to hide in a little glass house called science thinking it is an impenetrable fortress and throw bricks at the great greenhouses of religion. Has reason and rationality dealt with the abuse of power, the rape of the planet or unlocked the secrets of death?*

That's the Great Journey; yes religions have turned that journey into a stick to beat good people with. But if you throw out the baby with the bath water you are in danger of being as blind as many of those you despise. Remember it is very easy to become what you hate.'

Love is the Essence A Roman Catholic Bishop was in the crowd, he had challenged his colleagues over the child abuse scandal asking them to make a public, no holds barred apology. He had given a press conference at which he suggested that the Pope should give up his white robes from now until he dies and wear a simple black cassock. This, he said would at least give some symbol of sorrow. He also suggested the sale of the Church's assets to compensate victims. He had been ostracised by many in the Church hierarchy. But Jess had fascinated him and now he asked her a question:

'Miss Jess, what do you think matters most in life?'

Jess looked him in eye for a long time and then answered:

'Love, and by love I mean a willingness to go beyond, beyond judgement, beyond prejudice, beyond self protection, beyond being nice, beyond so called security, the love that you feel when you hold your new born child in your arms and think you would die for this little life.'

She paused,

'If we could treat each other with that tough and uncompromising love and offer it, especially to the most vulnerable be it people, animals or the planet itself, then we would be in tune with the very reason for our existence.'

The Bishop sighed replying,

'What you have said is so right. Love is the essence; I would say that God is love and that when you love you are one with God. We have forgotten in the Church what true love is, thinking that we are the only path to salvation when real love, wherever it is manifested is a gateway to true life. Love is treating the wounds of the victims and disarming the system and the individuals that cause all this pain.'

Jess was taken aback;

'I use the word love because God has become such a misused word it is almost meaningless, love is an active thing, permeating and surrounding us, it is the lever to change the world, the very life blood of the Great Turning and you are part of that Great Emergence when you act as you do.'

The session ended and many of the press ran off to file stories, as Saint Paul's had become a huge focus of media attention, though not that many read about it as they observed the fast. The government and other politicians were sending more and more people to listen and report back to them. The security services had her and her friends under surveillance and some corporations were paying private detectives and others to investigate her, as they perceived she was a growing threat.

There is an Alternative The weather was unseasonably warm so she took up a spot in Trafalgar Square and began to speak to the crowds using a public address system some of her helpers had hired.

'You have been told, over and over again, that there is no alternative to the system; the very system that is depriving millions of even the basics of life; the very system that is destroying that life giving complexity called planet earth; the very system that says things and the buying and selling of things matter more than the well being and happiness of people.

I am here to tell you that with all the creativity and imagination we have as humans there is definitely an alternative. The problem is that the system cannot stand a rival and will release antibodies to kill off any threat. These antibodies are called corporations and institutions that seek to keep a small group in power and work night and day to convince you that they are the only way.'

The crowd cheered and clapped. Those present were from all walks of life and represented a great cross section of the country. A fact not missed by those beginning to mass against Jess and her work.

Privilege is Blindness *'You see'* she continued, *'it is all a matter of perspective, the point from which you view this world we live in. Edlington gives you a special point of view! If you have always been at the top of the pile, been to the best schools, attended the cream of the country's universities, mixed with people who are just like you then that shapes what you see.*

If you don't know what a job centre smells like, what it is like to have to take food out of a shopping basket and put it back on the shelf, what cheap shoes feel like, or the look in a child's eyes when you tell them you can't afford their dreams then what qualifies you to be in charge?

Just watch those who are in charge, the wealthy, the influential, and the privileged. Unless they can free themselves from the blindness that being at the top of the system causes they are capable of the most horrendous atrocities without noticing the damage.

And worse even than that, is they've convinced all of us that this is the only way things can be! Made us feel so ignorant that we daren't challenge it, better to watch TV and play games than go on the Great Journey that will bring in the Republic of Hope.

The Great Journey requires new eyes, but this new seeing is hardest for those with the most to lose.'

Twisted Signposts

Thirteenth
Blog
London
April
2012

The Manager invited her into one of the cinemas in Leicester Square, he was completely captivated by her way of speaking but he had noticed that the Police were beginning to get twitchy about the size of the crowd. By now all kinds of groups were attaching themselves to the fringes of her gatherings, Anarchists and Socialist Workers, and there had been a few skirmishes. The Manager wanted the ordinary people to hear her unmolested (in fact he lost his job for his trouble).

Inside the cinema she told them a story.

'Today I sat with a woman in Westminster Cathedral, to most people she is just another Bag Lady but I had taken the trouble to get to know her. She uses her pension money everyday, to buy a homeless person a meal. She finds one, takes them to a café and sits with them and they eat together. She spends the whole time whilst they are eating listening whilst they tell her their story.

Now that's what I call giving, and let me tell you those so called religious leaders didn't even notice her when I took them to her and sat right next to her. There are none so blind as those who will not see!'

Someone in the cinema said,

'But surely those Churches are there to give glory to God, can't you see that, all over London, a great testament to faith?'

Jess countered,

'All I can see is that these buildings so easily get in the way. What that woman does is a testament to the Great Turning, it is levering it into this broken world, the buildings are at best signposts but even the best sign can end up twisted and pointing in the wrong direction. They will end in rubble, her act is written in another person's heart, that's indelible.'

The impromptu cinema session *The Tsunami to Come* ended and they returned to Saint Paul's. Jess and her close friends and helpers went around thanking everyone for their hard work as the three days of action came to an end. Many of the people who had become engaged in the action begged her to carry on. She told them that more was to come but this moment was over and she recognised many of them had families and work to go back to.

'This is like when the sea recedes before a Tsunami, we have only experienced the lapping of the ocean of change soon it will become a tidal wave. You all need to wait, look out for the signs, and be ready to act.'

Many ignored her instructions and kept up the occupation of the Cathedral and other parts of the City, much to the anger of the authorities. The Church leaders initiated Court action to have them forcibly removed.

Jess took her followers back to the East End *A Forest Fire* where they had been staying. Her closest friends, as they were eating a supper provided by a generous Bangladeshi Family in a café just off Brick Lane, asked her,

'How are we to know that the Great Turning is really starting, what did you mean look out for the signs?'

The meal had finished and they were all relaxed waiting eagerly to hear more from Jess, she settled in her chair and began,

'This is the Great Challenge to open the eyes of the soul and see what is really going on. So many people are full of predictions, fundamentalists of every kind claiming that this event or that portent marks the beginning of some awful apocalypse.

Some of them even put money into the state of Israel so that some fancy biblical geography is fulfilled and the so-called rapture will come. Others fly planes into towers, all of them think destruction is the gateway to change.

They couldn't be more wrong.

The Great Turning is a quiet revolution. The signs are more subtle. The whole system is falling apart, becoming more and more self-destructive and creating more and more victims who often believe they are powerless to do anything about it.

It is like looking at a great forest fire raging, it appears to destroy everything in its path and leaves behind a burnt and barren wilderness. The fall of the great system is just like this. But in fact when the fires have gone everything comes back to life, it needed this calamity in order to grow again. So we need this burning, then all those seeds that can withstand a flaming inferno will burst into life and give birth to a whole new world.

The problem at the moment is that those in power will not accept that the fire has come and keep trying to ignore the smell of burning. But if you are prepared to look the burnt wilderness head on you will see the shoots of a completely new forest.'

They all looked at one another, murmuring and *Love Wins* whispering. Confused, Jeff spoke up,

'What about us, is what we have been doing over the past three days part of this new forest?'

She turned to them all with a deeply serious look on her face.

'Yes it is, these moments are like birth pangs, you see the possibility of change, but be warned the labour could be long and hard. You will need to have courage. It is a fight because those who are in power do not want to see the world in any other way but their own and they spend a lot of time and energy trying to make the rest of us see it that way too.

If you keep on with this Great Turning then it will challenge their power and you may want to fight back with the same weapons they use. You can't because then you will be no different to them.

You must use the weapons of love and silence; actions are far more powerful than all the newspapers and TV stations in the world. Show people it is possible and without violence refuse to submit to their view. Live differently; in your heads and hearts, that is where the system cannot touch you if you don't let it in.

You will find yourselves on the wrong side of the all the powers in the world and they will attack you, but remember, and you will see me prove this very soon, love wins, just be sure you know what love is.'

Bounty asked her:

'How will we know when the Great Change is really happening?'

Stay True
Stay Awake
Stay Firm
Change will
Come

Jess thought for a while and they suspected she might not answer then she suddenly spoke again,

'There are some lies that when you hear them you will know that the system is about to collapse. When they say that war is peace making, when they say that torture is anti-terrorism, that privilege is an inherent right, that poverty and starvation are just the way things are, that in the real world all these lies are just normality, then you will know insanity has become acceptable. You know what you must do, make your lives say there is something better or get out and find other places where you can live a sane life.'

'You will need to stay awake, there are so many forces out there that want to put you back to sleep. Watch the adverts on TV, the Games, the Shows, the Blockbuster Movies, and of course those great fears—growing old, terrorism, having too little, getting too fat, foreigners, benefit cheats.

If you are awake you will be able to separate the sleeping tablet stuff from the stuff that sparks the Great Awakening. Believe me there are some films and stories that are break-through moments for the Turning, always they emerge when we need them. Once you wake up it is frightening to see how many are asleep in their lives!'

'There will be many more calamities and disasters, many have still to get the message. The environment cannot take the way we live, we are part of that, we kid ourselves we are not animals, not part of nature but we are and we depend on it to sustain us. It will turn on us for a while and this will seem like the end of the world but stay firm and finally the message will sink in. Many will rise up then and take charge and you will be amazed at what humanity is capable of'.

'Those that are on top now are in for such a fall, and those who are side-lined and ridiculed will suddenly find themselves asked to lead, if they have not been eradicated. You will think that the world as you know it is ending, that is when real faith is essential, not in doctrines or atheisms but the deepest kind of faith, faith in the holding that supports all reality, it does not matter what you call it, but when you are in most need you find it is there.'

Plots within Plots The three days of action had completely rattled the powers that be, so much so that the vested interests that hide behind governments and the markets were stung into action. They realised that the Church leaders and even many elected politicians would not have the courage to do what was needed. They decided it was time to do away with Jess Jennings once and for all.

It leaked out afterwards that a group of very wealthy and influential people hatched a plot launching the secret services of Britain and America to act on their behalf. They knew they could hide behind the more visible powers and in fact use them. These were only rumours and of course all shrouded in plausible deniability.

The covert operatives advised that it would have to be done in a more private place, not where she would be in a crowd who might riot. Easter was coming and they said that the evening before the Bank Holiday would be an optimum time. She was due, the next day, to address a huge rally in Hyde Park to announce the next phase of her Action for Change, as she called it. They decided to try and take her when she was with a small group that could be intimidated and could be kept quiet for a short time.

Jess had gone to stay at the house of Jackson the Dealer; he was an afro-Caribbean drug seller from Hackney and was now involved with Jess's movement. Over the last few days he had listened to her and was trying to get clean and change his way of life. Many were shocked that she would stay with him, right in the middle of a very rough estate in Hackney, but he had invited her and she was touched by his generosity.

At Jackson's Flat

He found places to put up Jess's friends, all around the area. They were preparing for the next part of the Action for Change and had stopped to eat a meal. An Asian man came in, no one was sure who had invited him. He went over to Jess and gave her a beautifully wrapped parcel. He said that she had really touched his heart with her words and actions and he wanted to give her a gift to thank her. Jess opened the box and took out the most exquisite Sari made of hand printed silk. As she wrapped the scarf around her neck some of the guests began to mutter to each other:

'I can't believe she has accepted that gift, she could sell it and give the money to a charity.'

Another said

'I bet he is trying to bribe her to do something for him, she's just like all these do gooders, only in it for herself.'

Many of the hangers on that had begun to surround her had invited themselves to the impromptu party, they scolded the man and told him to go on his way and leave Jess alone.

She heard this and said

'Why do you react from some script you have playing in your heads and not look at things as they are, right in front of your noses. He has done me a great kindness, this is a beautiful gift given with grace, and that is how I am going to accept it, with grace. When I go through death I want to wear this in memory of all the beauty and kindness I have seen in the world.'

Davina's Weakness The Secret Services had in fact been aware of Jess and her activities for some time and had made a number of attempts to infiltrate her movement. The problem was that she had created no recognisable hierarchy, so it was very difficult to find any inner circle. However the people she had begun with in Edlington were very often with her and coordinated much of the work, so efforts were made to investigate their backgrounds and then covertly contact them to see if any weaknesses could be exploited.

The media, especially the tabloid newspapers, were making all kinds of offers and enticements to people close to Jess in order to gain information. They hacked phones and computers as well as raking through Jess's past for anything that could be printed. Many of the editors and owners were furious with her unwillingness to give interviews and her overt and constant criticism of them.

Davina one of Jess's original friends had been involved in benefit fraud and never been caught. A journalist discovered this and used it to get some information about the group and Jess's plans. The journalist had passed her name to a senior police officer in the Met and from there it found its way to the Secret Services.

A Final Meal Davina was taken by an operative to a secret location and interrogated, the benefit fraud was used to soften her up and then sweeteners were offered. She succumbed and agreed to use a mobile phone they gave her to let them know where Jess would be on Easter Sunday evening and how many people were around her. They told her that they only wanted to get Jess off the streets and give her the chance to explain her ideas.

A couple of Jess's friends asked her

'Where are we going to eat tonight, do you want to stay here with Jackson again or what?'

Jess answered

'I have made arrangements with a man called Rahman Chowdhury he will be waiting for you at the top of Brick Lane and will take you to his restaurant on Princelet Street. Tell him we will be there at eight.'

They went and found the man waiting and found the restaurant as she had said. It was closed to the public and made ready for a private meal. At eight she arrived with the rest of her closest friends including Davina. The meal was fantastic, a banquet with all the trimmings. They were all surprised as she usually ate simply and always just what their host offered. This evening seemed to have been arranged well in advance and the menu agreed with many special dishes.

Halfway through the meal she suddenly seemed really upset and made a surprising announcement.

'One of you sitting round the table is going to give me away to the authorities. I know you don't mean to hurt me and you think you are protecting yourself but believe me the consequences will be more far reaching than you expect.'

They all looked around at each other in horror. Many of them offered assurances that they would never do some thing like that, Davina, however kept quiet but Jess met her eyes and she looked away after a few seconds.

Before they could ask any more questions Jess changed the subject. They were all aware that she was not herself and that she had much on her mind. All through what had a been a wonderful meal she had seemed distracted and she now began to say and do things that made them really sit up and take notice.

She had asked the restaurant staff to bring in some bottles of wine at the end of the meal and she also had saved a bowl of chapattis from the main course. She began to pour the wine into cups and tear the bread up into pieces. Then she began to speak to them,

'Many of you have seen these symbols in churches, some of you have been to services where they have been shared. They have become so familiar and institutionalised that most people have forgotten what they really mean.'

They stared at her and each other feeling totally confused.

'The bread is the same bread that the children of Israel took from their captivity in Egypt, the bread of the dispossessed, even in the camps of the holocaust they tried to eat it. It made them part of a story, one body with all the lost, poor and broken of the world. This bread in my hands made by Muslims, is a staple, always the poorest turn to the simplest of ingredients to keep body and soul together. It is seed, sown and harvested, crushed and baked. It is everyone who has been through the mill. I am about to go through my own mill and you will have your own crushing. When we share it we become part of the great story and one with the body of humanity suffering and tortured and the eating should make us more willing to go through it so a better world can be born.'

She gave the bread out and they ate it together with her. She opened the wine and poured it in to their cups.

'This wine has been crushed too. It has been fermented and allowed to produce a dangerous and powerful spirit. We drink it to remember, to forget, when we want to celebrate our relationships, marriages, births, deaths. We save it up for special times and share it with each other. It is poured

out, as we are when we love, when we don't hold back but give ourselves. How many stories are there of one person sacrificing themselves for another to save them? When we drink this we are saying yes to that love. Yes to life, even at the cost of our own.'

She encouraged them to drink and enjoy the wine. She asked them all to name someone they would want to give life to. For some it was children, or parents, or partners, for others the many people they had encountered in their work with her.

'So many churches have turned this simple act into some solemnity that can only be done by certain people and only in sacred buildings. So often the simple, liberating truth has been turned by religion into something that only the chosen can do and the rest have to follow behind and do what they are told. They have even turned the most profound act of self-giving into a ceremony that is used to exclude people because they don't live up to the standards of the sacred cast, standards they don't even practice themselves.

We eat to remember and to be brought together in our willingness to change the world and to do it with our love. If you had eyes to see you would see it is happening all the time all over the world. The single Mother giving her children beans on toast is a breaking and her crushing will change her and the kids through her love. Do this to change yourselves and the world, that is the only obligation I give you.'

Her close friends all sat there completely dumfounded, wondering what she was talking about, why was she so sombre? It seemed as if she were making some kind of farewell, whereas they all felt things were just about to go to another level. They left the restaurant and she took them to an open space at the bottom of Brick Lane called Altab Ali Park.

The Shade of my Tree They sat around the Shaheed Minar, a memorial to the Bangladeshi Language Movement and she spoke to them again.

'This park remembers Altab Ali, a young Bangladeshi man murdered in this area because he was Asian, also you can see the shape of the old Church etched into the ground, it was bombed in the Blitz. This place shows that it is not race or religion that causes evil but poverty and those in power holding on to it at any cost.

I am about to be taken away from you and you will all feel like your lives have fallen apart. You will want to blame me. But I have kept trying to tell you it has to be this way, so I can prove that love is stronger than evil. But when I reappear I will go back to Edlington, look for me there'.

Rob stood up, looking down at her, *'Even if all the rest of these nesh out*[11] *I will stay with you.'*

Jess stood and faced him, putting her hand on his shoulder,

'Don't be so cocky, this is harder than you think, I tell you that tonight before the sun comes up again you will have disowned me and everything I stand for.'

'No chance' he shouted at her *'even if I have to fight to the death I will protect you'.*

'I want no one to kill for me, it is dying that changes things not killing',

Jess replied.

They all protested that they were willing to die for the cause and she smiled ruefully at them and sat down again.

She pointed out to them that there were words
Weariness written on the path; *"The shade of my tree is offered to those who come and go fleetingly,"* she told them *'these are the words of Tagore a Bengali Poet and they are comforting to me now.'*

They wondered, as they often did how she knew all these things. Before they could ask her she said,

---

[11] A South Yorkshire expression for running away.

'I need to be silent for a while, I am going under those trees, make sure I am not disturbed and stay awake as I want to know when the time comes.'

They wondered what she meant but they daren't ask and just sat a way off gradually dozing off. Davina said she needed to find a loo and went off down the street. She texted the number the secret services had given her and told them that Jess was in a quiet place with few people around. She came back before they could suspect her of anything.

Jess came closer to them after half an hour and found them dozing.

'This is going to be the hardest night of our lives, can't you at least keep yours eyes open?' She poked them all awake as she said this.

Rob, Julie and Jeff went and sat closer to her and tried to stay awake, it was a warm evening for the time of year so it was hard. They heard her speaking out loud. She kept saying the same phrase over and over,

'Forgive me my weariness, O Lord. Should I ever lag behind, for this heart that this day trembles so?'[12]

She was shaking and crying and when she came back to them they were all asleep again.

She pulled them upright; *'Have I taught you nothing if you don't find the inner silence how will you stand up to what is coming?'*

They looked sheepish and protested that they would watch from then on. They could see she was upset and tried to get her to move on and go back to Jackson's place. She just went back to the trees and sat in silence again. Again murmuring the same verses, shivering and moaning. After some minutes their eyes drooped again. Finally she came back to them and woke them gently and took them back to the others and woke them too. Davina was missing and they all wondered where she might have gone.

---

[12] A quote from Tagore

Suddenly dark figures stole in through *Taken in the Dark* the gates with Davina behind them trying to keep out of sight. Dressed in black military uniforms with automatic weapons and bulletproof vests they were in full operational mode, moving from cover to cover. One of them turned to Davina and whispered;

'*Which one is Jennings?*'

Davina pointed to Jess and they swarmed towards her, grabbing her wrists, using plastic tags to bind her. Her comrades especially the men tried to resist, Kumar grabbed one of the operatives and tried to wrestle the gun from him. The operative smashed him in the jaw and sent him sprawling, blood pouring from his nose and mouth.

Jess intervened, '*No violence, remember we will die but never kill.*'

Her friends backed away as the operatives trained their weapons on them. The leader spoke,

'*We have what we came for so you had better run or we'll take you as well.*'

She spoke to the operative

'*All this time I have acted in public and you never came near me only now in the dark do you choose to take me.*'

He responded by slapping her, gagging her and then turning his weapon towards her friends. That was the final straw they fled in terror running in different directions.

There was one journalist who had been allowed to be with her from the beginning and was just coming into the park to speak with her. He had been interviewing the restaurant owner and grabbed his camera and tried to take some pictures. One of the men in black caught sight of him and ran after him, catching him just at the entrance, bringing him down, grabbing the camera and wrestling with him for possession of it. The journalist ran for his life leaving the camera in the hands of the operative.

With great haste she was driven to *The Archbishop's Palace* Lambeth Palace in an unmarked black van. Rob had hung around and grabbed a taxi telling it to follow the van, arriving just behind them; he then loitered outside the gates.

Agents from both sides of the Atlantic were involved, shadowy figures representing even more shadowy vested interests. They had insisted that the first interrogation of Jess take place at the Primate's Palace and the Archbishop found this hard to resist, as it was his task force that had originally looked into her case and the government insisted this was initially, a church matter. He was however terribly perplexed when he realised the nature of her arrest and the forces that seemed to be behind it.

Moreover, he had the more conservative wing of the Church of England baying for her blood. The evangelicals considered her non biblical and being a woman made her very unpopular with the Anglo-Catholic wing. Even the Roman Catholic Bishops (in general) were furious about what they perceived to be her attacks on Catholicism and Church order. It was the leaders of the Churches who had approached the government about her activities at St Paul's. They wanted help to have her and her activists moved on. Furthermore they were all deeply troubled about the next phase of her action, they had come out of the Three Days of Action badly and the last thing they wanted was more of the same.

The Archbishop obviously wanted to do the right thing and had called senior synod members to his palace along with some of the leaders of other churches. They were all very flustered at having to come out so late. It was, by then, eleven thirty in the evening. When she was brought in under guard and in restraints they were even more alarmed. The Government had sent a senior advisor from the office of the Home Secretary and the Archbishop asked why the need for such heavy handed treatment. He was told that Jess was considered a major security risk because of the groups she was involved with, Al Qaeda was mentioned in hushed tones.

Also present were some of the original members of the fact-finding mission that had been investigating her activities in South Yorkshire as well as others from the delegation sent by the secret summit. Selected journalists were there too, those that the Secret Services deemed appropriate, who would put the right spin on any story they printed. They had already been very helpful in hacking phones and email accounts to produce the (so-called) evidence to be deployed against Jess now.

The Archbishop and the Church Leaders sat behind a great table surrounded variously by their staff and advisors; behind them were the Government representatives and Secret Service minders. Jess was alone behind a small table in front of them.

The restaurant owner on hearing of her arrest from the journalist had managed to contact a Lawyer from the Tower Hamlets Law Centre. The lawyer, a black African woman, was a specialist in human rights and had represented many ethnic minority clients in East London, victims of racism, wrongful arrest and other forms of discrimination. She had heard of Jess but never met her until this evening. She swept in past the security guards and minions in the Archbishop's Palace with such authority that they allowed her to sit down next to Jess.

Jess was accused of a variety of heresies and theological inconsistencies; her acceptance of gay marriage was examined, her negative attitude to Church authority was questioned and she was challenged about what the investigation called her relativist approach to the uniqueness of Christianity in relation to what she called the Great Emergence, especially during her three days of action. These among many other ecclesiastical niceties were levelled at her and to all she made little reply, except to comment that if they had a problem with her why don't they take it up with the thousands who seemed to agree with her. This incensed many of her opponents who came up with more and more outrageous charges.

Wincing and Shifting The lawyer intervened at this point, asking about the legal status of the hearing and what right they had to arrest and detain her client. Her name was Josephine Akubu and she spoke now with such authority, the authority that comes from within not just from letters after a name, that the Archbishop felt compelled to answer. Jess sat motionless.

'I am sorry Ms . . . .'

'Akubu, Josephine Akubu of the Tower Hamlets Law Centre'.

'Well Ms Akubu, this is an informal hearing. Ms Jennings, whom you claim to represent, has stirred up a huge amount of controversy both for the Church and the Country as a whole and we wanted to establish the facts so that this can all be discussed in Synod in the proper manner.'

Jess suddenly stirred.

'I have been available to come and speak to you any time you wanted, all you had to do was ask. Yet you come and arrest me in the dark, with few around and with what seemed to be some secret tactical unit from who knows where.'

The Archbishop winced, and shifted in his seat.

'The manner of your apprehension was not my choice' he glanced at the dark suited advisor, *'I agree it is regrettable and I have asked that you be released from the restraints and I ask that again.'*

This time the dark suited man nodded to one of the operatives who came and cut the wrist restraints.

Josephine stood and addressed the gathered men and women facing her.

'My client has never expressed any allegiance or sought membership of any of the Churches represented here and she has never done anything violent. She has sought to communicate with many people and always done so in public or on open websites. What possible threat does she pose to National Security or Church order?'

The Archbishop hesitated and then the Catholic Cardinal leant over to him and whispered to him for some while. The Archbishop recoiled from the conversation as if he had touched a live wire. He leant across to one of the leading evangelical priests who had massive congregations across the country and had been one of Jess's most outspoken critics. Again the Archbishop shrunk back from the prelate.

Slowly, drawing himself up in the seat he seemed to make a decision. He faced Jess and asked

'We have heard rumours from many sources that those who go around with you and others you have had contact with believe, and I hardly dare say it as it seems so ridiculous, that you think you are Jesus Christ the Son of God somehow returned. Theologically this is madness,' he looked at the Evangelical Priest and the Cardinal as he said this, *'but I have to ask you is that who you think you are?'*

There was a long drawn out silence, the air became thick with expectation.

'Yes I am.' She said in such a way that the words hung in the air for a few moments. *'To see me in action is to see the truth he brought active again in a world that seems to have largely forgotten what he came for'.*

The Evangelical Priest leapt to his feet demanding

'For goodness sake do we need to listen to any more, she has hanged herself with her own words, how on earth could the Lord Jesus have anything to do with this woman. "Many will come in my name saying I am he" Mark thirteen-six, she is either mad or very dangerous either way she must be stopped, what are you going to do Archbishop convene another committee?'

The Catholic Bishops and the Cardinal were nodding and all the Church representatives were unanimous in their condemnation.

The Archbishop made one final attempt.

'You mean surely that you believe you are acting in Christ's spirit? Don't you realise that Christ gave us the Church to lead us in faith and guide our actions.'

'Don't answer that' Josephine intervened *'these people are just out to incriminate you one way or another',*

Jess put her hand on the Lawyers shoulder and smiled, she rose to her feet

'The Great Change that Jesus embodied is embodied in me too.

It is embodied in all those who are willing to turn towards it like a ship turning into the wind.

You have all forgotten what a wild and untamed spirit that wind is.

I have come to take everything this suicidal system can throw at me.

Jesus is not a religion, he came to put an end to your way of doing things, if you want to be part of the Great Turning you don't worship Jesus you live him.

The thing that saddens me most is that you and all of your colleagues have joined the system and then you call that collusion service, when it is really self-preservation and the preservation of your positions at the top of the system with all the power, privilege and prestige that gives you.

The Great Emergence does not need your institutions in fact most of the time they block it.

I am here to serve notice that the Great Turning will undermine, from the inside the whole rotten system and believe me, the love that drives that Change cannot be snuffed out.'

The Archbishop who always tried to be fair slumped in his chair defeated. The people around him leant into a huddle and after a moment he raised his hand.

'I had hoped to find a way to have you released, to give evidence to the synod at a later date but my hands are tied. Your claims put you beyond the Church's authority; it is as my esteemed colleagues say absolutely unorthodox to do and say what you have. I do not believe you are the threat to national security the government say you are but you are a threat to the good honest faith of our people. As such I must declare you barred from any Church under my jurisdiction, you cannot speak on our property and we denounce your work'.

One by one the other leaders stood up and said much the same. The government's advisor on National Security concluded the proceedings by thanking the Archbishop for his hospitality and help in flushing out such a dangerous person. He declared that Jess would be taken to the Houses of Parliament to go before a hastily convened Intelligence and Security Select Committee to answer charges of inciting terrorism.

They replaced the restraints around Jess's wrists and dragged her out towards the entrance, Josephine following right behind insisting on accompanying her.

By now it had become known that Jess had been arrested and a crowd had gathered on the road outside the Palace gatehouse. Though all her close friends had dispersed and were hiding, Rob had followed her. He was in the front of the crowd. A woman in the throng who had been part of the campaign at St Paul's saw him and pushed her way to him grabbing his shoulder.

'*Rob*' she shouted '*what's going on, where is she?*'

At that moment the blacked out security van carrying Jess swept past, one of the out-riders stopped in front of Rob staring at him.

'*I don't know I'm not part of this, I was just walking past*' Rob answered the woman, never looking at her but staring at the ground.

'*You are, I saw you there at the camp, every day. Anyway listen to your voice, you are from the North and she brought you all down with her.*' The woman was completely certain.

The rider had stopped and taken his helmet off. Rob recognised him as one of the operatives who had been at Altab Ali Park. He looked straight at Rob, and spoke in a menacing voice;

'Well, are you one of hers? You look familiar to me and I have orders to arrest any one in this crowd who was close to her.'

'For fuck's sake what's wrong with you all, can't a bloke from the north walk the streets of London. I have no idea who you are talking about I have come looking for work, and I am staying with a mate round the corner.'

Just then another bike came past, stopped and called the rider to hurry up. He shrugged and got back on his bike. The woman looked at Rob with disgust on her face and turned away. Rob ran off, broken and ashamed.

Jess Against the World With high security and great haste Jess was whisked over to the Houses of Parliament and placed in a secure room guarded by operatives and forbidden any visitors. Josephine Akubu had been prevented from accompanying Jess on her short journey and was, even at that moment, seeking a judicial ruling allowing her to represent Jess at the hearing.

The city was quiet, being early on an Easter Bank Holiday morning. It was proving very difficult to convene the committee and some members were away. They had been contacted the evening before and those from the government side had received personal calls from the Home Secretary demanding their presence.

The committee was finally quorate at 9.15am and met in camera, that is in private with no public or press presence permitted. Josephine had finally persuaded a judge to rule on her representation of Jess, he had reluctantly admitted that she was within her remit to be present. When she arrived she found three National Security advisers were presenting the case against her client.

Jess was ushered in, again handcuffed and looking the worse for wear. She had obviously been interrogated and some physical coercion had been exerted. She was limping and her face was puffy and her right eye was swollen.

The Chair of the committee was a previous Home Secretary and had been well briefed. It was crucial, he had been told, that they establish Jess as a major threat to national security and that she should be interned under the Anti Terrorism Act.

Again Josephine attempted to ascertain the legal status of the committee and was informed that it was a matter of national security and that the committee had been convened in order to give an immediate judgement to the Home Secretary on the level of threat posed and what remedy was necessary.

'*She is not a disease she is a human being*' Josephine quipped.

'*Please Ms Akubu we are not here to bandy words with an ill informed solicitor, we have a major threat to our way of life to deal with. The quicker you allow us to get on with it, the better for all of us.*' replied the Chair.

The evidence against her went on for over an hour. The charges ranged from her trying to hack into and subvert the stock market mainframes to a plot to bomb major sporting venues, one being the new Olympic stadium on the day of the opening ceremony.

Jess made no answer to any of their claims. She sat impassive and even when Josephine attempted to persuade her to speak she remained silent. The Chair of the Committee, sensing time passing and fearing that her supporters would be organising themselves, moved in for the kill.

'*Is it the case that you have advocated the complete overturning of the state and following your violent revolution a new order where people's legitimate rights to their wealth and status be stripped from them?*'

Jess finally broke her silence;

'*You need to work that out for yourself sir*' she said with a quiet determination '*I have kept none of my work secret, you can Google me, you can talk to those who listened to me and followed my way, you can see the fruit of my work and that will tell you all you want to know'.*

The Chairman of the Committee, Michael Parton-Stuart was a man used to being respected and fawned upon, this answer incensed him, yet recognising that all eyes were on him he called for a pause in proceedings. He wanted to call the Home Secretary and get her advice as to how to proceed. She advised him to grab the senior opposition MP, one Giovanna Bacelli. She was very ambitious and had been tipped for a senior shadow cabinet post in the next reshuffle. She had a media background having been a senior news editor for Sky News, Parton-Stuart took her to one side.

'Both sides of the house agree that this woman is trouble and needs to be taken off the streets as soon as possible'. He began.

She nodded, *'How about using some of your friends in the press to win a few hearts and minds to our cause. I can be very useful to your career Giovanna, I know I am on the other side and all that, but really the greasy pole is the same either side of this house and there is a large dash of kudos in this for you.'*

'Okay I think I can handle this. It'll take a couple of hours.'

'Right I will adjourn till lunch and then we will see how the land lies'.

He turned on his heel and she sped off already dialling the first contact she was to exploit.

She returned to Parton-Stuart's offices after around ninety minutes.

'Okay I have a proposition for you, you won't like it, but it will work, I guarantee it.'

'I'm listening' he replied

'Okay, you know the al-Qaeda cleric you have under high security arrest at the moment'

'Yes' he said frowning.

'*And you know the European tribunal thinks you should release him because he can't be extradited for fear he won't get a fair trial in Israel.*'

The chairman leaned forward nodding,

'*Well release him, now, this afternoon. The press will go crazy, the left will be caught out as the human rights of a fermenter of terrorism isn't what they had in mind when they bang on about liberty, your back benchers will be able to point to the excesses of Europe and the government will be able to say their hands were tied. No one will be interested in some Hairdresser's daughter from South Yorkshire when this breaks. You can do what you like with her for a couple of days and no one will notice*'.

Parton-Stuart looked dubious, suspicious that this was some plot within a plot, so he pondered for a minute and then said,

'*You are in the wrong party girl, we could do with a few more like you on our side who know how to cut to the chase to protect the good honest folk of this great nation.*' He laughed.

'*Sitting opposite you doesn't mean we don't know a real threat when we see one, and that woman is dangerous because she can't be bought.*' Giovanna retorted.

He dismissed her with a promise of patronage and favour and then whisking out his mobile phone proceeded to persuade the Home Secretary of the twisted yet inexorable logic of the plan. Finally she agreed and set the wheels in motion for a bank holiday release. The Home Secretary's addition to the plan was that the release would in fact only be a sham and the man would be quickly placed under house arrest and tagged, just as soon as the press could be diverted to some other carefully spun issue. They would find a way to bring him to justice before the next election. Parton-Stuart, of course failed to mention the originator of the plan and basked in the credit he received.

Spirited Away As expected the release unleashed a media storm. The journalists covering Jess' case were all diverted to the story, leaving the committee free to finally determine that Jess was a threat to national security and should be retained in the custody of the security services.

While the media were occupied waiting outside the prison of the al-Qaeda cleric and awaiting the Home Secretary's hastily convened press conference, it was put out that Jess was to be taken away for further questioning. The Security Services used underground passageways in the Houses of Parliament to take her to an unmarked van and off to a secret location, a clandestine safe house in Pimlico. Josephine was also taken for questioning by the Security Services to another location thus nullifying her ability to alert Jess' friends and supporters as to her whereabouts or even the outcome of proceedings. All means of communication were removed from her.

Plausible Denial The dark forces behind the elected officials now had a free hand. It had been determined that she was to be terminated in such a way that plausible denial could always be maintained by all those involved.

The cabal of wealthy, influential and unelected leaders had seen to it that the Prime Minister had abdicated final responsibility for her fate to the head of the special operations in consort with CIA so that he could maintain ignorance of the affair. The American president's security advisors kept him abreast of this but without any paper trail or traceable lines of communication.

Tortured Yet Silent Hooded and handcuffed for the journey, she arrived at the safe house and was made to stand in stress positions whilst remaining blindfolded, ears plugged and mouth gagged. They were determined to find out if she had any connections with other groups or if she had been recruited to carry out her operations by known terrorist organisations.

She was kept that way for most of the night. The sensory deprivation was broken only by her being dragged into an intensely lit room and subjected to questioning interspersed with periods of agonisingly loud white noise, all the while hanging by her wrists, feet just grazing the floor.

She made no response to their repeated questioning, which only served to infuriate her captors all the more. They finally resorted to water boarding, an horrific practice where the victim is pinned on her back with head inclined downwards, her face is covered with a porous cloth, water is then poured in great amounts over the victim's face. This induces the sensation of drowning and can induce terrible panic sometimes even leading to heart failure.

She kept, through all this horror, a stubborn and dignified silence. Having passed out three times during the water boarding, when they revived her the third time she collapsed into tears and curled up onto the floor of her cell in a foetal position. She had been stripped naked and threats of rape and abuse were hurled at her.

Then suddenly a new senior operative entered the room. He ordered her clothes to be found and after she was covered he made sure her wounds were dressed and offered her a cup of tea. She drank it thirstily having become, ironically after being covered in so much water, extremely dehydrated. Unknown to Jess the tea was drugged with a powerful hallucinogenic, often used, both to disorientate and elicit truth from a subject. She began to scream as the visual and auditory disturbances became more and more intense. After an hour of this the man was satisfied that she actually had no connections to other groups and was not working for *al-Qaeda*.

She was thrown back into her cell and allowed to sleep for a few hours. Throughout this the only response she would make to them was that she forgave them. One of the operatives found this both insufferable and yet also fascinating. He asked her why she said this.

'*Because you only know how to do what you are ordered to do, and you, all of you, are asleep in your lives; you only see what you are shown by those in power, this is the way it has always been.*'

He responded, '*You do know you are going to die very soon and that all your work will be forgotten by next month. If I was you I would be terrified and furious, doing all I could to get away.*'

'*You would only kill me sooner and say I was attempting to escape.*' Which was in fact one of their options.

'*My message, however is irrepressible and in fact the Great Emergence is only ushered in through forgiveness and reconciliation and love.*'

They then made her look reasonably presentable. Her mobile phone was then retrieved and they sent texts to two of her friends saying she had escaped and would meet them near a place on the Chelsea embankment near the Royal Hospital Grounds right next to the River Thames. The texts had just the right note of urgency and authenticity to convince them that the messages were real. The agreed time was two hours from then so the oncoming night would cover their activities.

The operatives drove her in an unmarked van, gagged and bound to the agreed spot. She was then unbound and drugged with a sedative that made her semi conscious. They carried her to the bank of the river, stripped her and placed her phone and clothes in a pile on the bank.

They had set the phone to send more texts to her close friends saying that she had named them all to the security services as traitors and terrorists and that she felt so wracked with guilt for giving them away that the only answer was to end it all. They had been very careful to make the wording so much in her style they would believe it.

Execution in a Civilised Society Other operatives had been very busy whilst Jess was held in the Safe House. They had again turned to their friends in the media. Davina had proved most cooperative and they had uncovered that Jess's Father had spent a few months in a psychiatric hospital when he was younger and made two suicide attempts. A story was published linking him with Jess' so called megalomania and an accompanying interview with a psychiatrist saying that often what accompanies great bouts of hubris and the cult of personality is an implosion when the perpetrator is found to be a charlatan leading to suicidal tendencies

Then three of the secret service personnel took nylon-covered weights and attached them to her legs and torso. Jess all through this process was awake enough to know what was happening to her but unable to move. They carried her out into the current of the river and threw her into the water. Rapidly her body was carried away as she slowly sank beneath the surface. Her lungs quickly filling with water, as she could do nothing to keep herself afloat, she was dead within minutes. They made sure that the place they dumped her was gravelly enough not to show any tracks.

It was crucial to the plan hatched by the dark forces ranged against Jess that there be no body to find. The fact that she had sunk without trace allowed them to leave the scene speedily, confident that all evidence of her would gradually decompose under the water.

No Story Like an Old Story It had been arranged that a local policeman would be sent to the spot a few minutes after the operatives had left so he could discover the evidence and be waiting for her friends when they arrived a few minutes later. The Police had just been informed of her escape from custody and were obviously not in on the subterfuge.

It happened that the Police Constable dispatched had heard Jess speak the week before and was quickly able to identify her stuff given that he found her clothes and the phone along with other cleverly placed identifying possessions, he immediately presumed suicide. This, as was intended, made the whole story all the more believable.

When Bethany and Bounty reached the place they found Constable Waring already going through Jess's belongings and informed him of the texts they had received. Grief engulfed them as they waited for the forensic team to arrive and began answering questions about what they knew. It wasn't long before the press were on the scene along with others of Jess's friends. A whole melee of people watched as the scene was marked off with incident tape by the authorities and statements were sought and given.

The story was rapidly reported that Jess had escaped Police custody earlier that morning and though an immediate search had been implemented, she had somehow slipped through the net. A man was found who claimed he had picked her up in his van in Pimlico and as he was going to make a delivery near the Royal Hospital she asked him to drop her off there. It was, initially, universally agreed that she had taken her own life. That being established a cursory search was made for the body and an inquest was opened and adjourned to a later date.

Suspicions But No Proof

Among Jess's friends and many of the Agents for Change there was huge consternation and despair. Many of them were utterly stunned and yet her closest friends remained unconvinced that she would take her own life. They suspected a plot against her by the highest powers but had no proof.

There had been an immediate crackdown on their activities, websites were closed down, offices raided and some of them had been arrested on Anti-Terrorism charges. A climate of fear pervaded their gatherings and her original friends were already planning to go back North and try to pick up the fragments of their lives.

Bethany and Bounty, however, were so suspicious of the circumstances surrounding Jess's disappearance that they decided to return to the scene. The fateful day had been the Tuesday after the Easter Bank Holiday, it was now Thursday and they were amazed how quickly the whole story had fallen out of the media spotlight. Even the story about the al-Qaeda suspect's release had been superseded by an alleged affair between a government minister and a male competitor on the X Factor, all the more juicy because he had just come out strongly against civil partnerships and gay marriage.

The two women had little idea of what they would find but they felt deeply drawn to return. When they arrived early in the morning the place seemed to have returned to normal. No police tape, no forensics tent, in fact no sign of the authorities at all. A hidden surveillance camera had been placed to view the site remotely, the operatives still being keen to cover all bases, but the women were not aware of it.

Figures in the Mist They wandered around, aimlessly for a few minutes sharing with each other their grief that there was no body to bury. They wondered about walking down the bank to see if there was any sign of Jess's remains.

Suddenly a figure emerged out of the hazy mist that lay around them and upon the river, they recognised him as the Policeman who had been at the scene on the day of Jess's disappearance. He was, however, off duty and wearing civilian clothing.

'What are you doing here' Bounty asked, expecting him to say that they should move on and that this was still a crime scene.

The man smiled and said,

'I came back here this morning, as I felt something urging me to return. I am deeply suspicious about the way it all went down on Tuesday. It was all too convenient and quickly tied up. Nothing is ever that simple. But that's not the point' He said with a strange look on his face that made the women very curious.

He led them back up to the park opposite the river and sat them down.

'She has reappeared' he said

'*What?*' They blurted out.

'*I was walking along the bank, up river about half an hour ago, looking for any signs that may have been missed. When to my astonishment she appeared out of the mist, walking towards me dressed in the most beautiful sari.*'

'*What you mean she didn't commit suicide after all?*' Bethany asked, incredulous.

'*No, weirder than that,*' he said earnestly, '*she told me the security forces had tortured her, drugged and then drowned her, but that there was a greater power in the world than theirs and she was evidence of that and you all should go back North and she would meet you there.*'

The two women stared in amazement at the Policeman wondering if he were trying to trick them or perhaps just had mental health issues. Yet he seemed both sane and deadly serious.

'*We should leave here*' he said having some sense that the scene would be watched. '*Let's go back to the bank quickly and see if she is still there*'.

They hurried down to the bank and strode into the mist. Sure enough she was there and she embraced the women with such love and warmth. They collapsed into her arms and sobbed as did Jess. After a few minutes of silent hugging and euphoria she told them to go and tell the others that she would meet them in Edlington. They parted and headed off towards the tube station together with the off duty constable who decided to travel North with them.

An Unexplained Fourth

He had been right about surveillance. As soon as the morning shift at the safe house saw the footage of the three of them talking so animatedly, they then rewound the recording to see them all disappear into the mist, their suspicions immediately aroused.

They headed straight down to the scene and found it deserted. All that they could make out in the muddy bank, where the tide had gone out were four sets of footprints. It confused them greatly and they could never account for the unknown fourth person in that early morning encounter.

Witnesses It became a red-hot issue in the days to come as rumours began to emerge that Jess had reappeared and had been seen by a number of people in Edlington. Accounts flew around the web, making all kinds of outlandish claims. That she had not committed suicide, that she had been tortured by the authorities, that her escape and subsequent death had been staged to look like suicide, that the government had been so threatened that it had been decided at the highest levels to dispose of her.

Outrageous Claims The most outrageous claims came from her closest friends. Rumours filtered out that they asserted she had in fact been murdered but that she had reappeared and spent time with them in Edlington. Grainy photos went up on Facebook and even a poor quality video was posted on YouTube claiming to show her sitting in a house in Edlington having a cup of tea and laughing.

Those closest to her continued her policy of never talking to the media and the posts never came from them but from people outside Jess's intimate circle.

The security forces tried to question many of them but they were very hard to pin down. All they would ever say was that they knew what had taken place and offered forgiveness on Jess's behalf and asked their questioners to leave their jobs and come and join the movement.

A Visible Reality The movement continued to bear many names, the Great Turning, the Great Emergence or the Great Peace and many others. All describing something organic and uncontrollable and this is what disturbed the powers that had conspired against her , the fact that they could not put a stop to it. The work seemed to have taken on a new lease of life since

Jess' murder. Her people were more organised and less hierarchical, actions springing up all over the place. Cells, as they called their little groups, were spreading to every town and the work initiated on those three days at St Paul's spread virally. What had begun, as one woman's mission to inaugurate the Great Emergence, was now becoming more and more a visible reality.

Afterword

When I was twenty, I worked in an unfashionable men's clothing shop called Ray Allan Manshops in the centre of Sheffield. It was my first job, the consequence of having failed miserably at school. It was the middle of a recession, jobs were not easy to come by, we were paid one percent commission on our sales and I earned marginally more than unemployment benefit. We sales assistants were regularly told by the our senior managers that there were a hundred people out there to take our jobs if we were daft enough to leave them or feckless enough to lose them.

One Friday the shop manager told us that a lad from his hometown of Maltby was starting as an assistant the next Monday, as an aside he cautioned us that he was one of those born again Christians, we had been warned. His name was Mick and in a disarming and unstereotypical way he was a punk, jet black dyed hair, Sid Vicious thin and at breaks chain smoking in the tea room. I awaited the evangelical persuasion, the sales pitch to save my soul. It never came. I became so curious that I finally asked him what was so good about Christianity.

I had no faith, having lost my Dad to a stroke and heart attack when I was eleven and then watched my Mum go through a nervous break down during my mid teens, I had rejected any possibility that there was a God. So I felt ready with a panoply of arguments that would soon wake him up to the harsh realities of my world. Unnervingly he seemed to be well aware of them, having grown up in a South Yorkshire pit village. So when he presented me with a small, well thumbed New Testament and told me if I wanted to see what Jesus was all about I should read Mark's Gospel, I had no idea what I was in for.

Any perceptions of Jesus I had were of the gentle, meek and mild variety. Just another part of the background furniture of my world, institutionally sterile. I sat that night on the bus home, surreptitiously reading the opening chapter of Mark, swept along by its breakneck pace, caught up with a character who was anything but institutional or sterile. By chapter three his enemies were plotting to kill him - I almost missed my stop, I was completely astonished.

I remain astonished. Astonished that, in general, many Christians have failed to present the character that stepped out of the little brown plastic bound bible on the number Seventeen bus in 1980. My journey to the centre of the Catholic Church and out again into a strange hinterland beyond institutional Christianity has convinced me that a predominantly churchless (or at least not institutionally controlled) way of accommodating the man and message contained in Mark's gospel is imperative. Imperative, that is, if the crisis and the challenges we are facing in the second decade of the 21st century are to be negotiated with courage, tenacity and creative ingenuity.

The Jesus imperative seems, to me, more about an unreserved personal renegotiation of the way we live our lives than the perpetuation of inward looking institutions that seek to impose a particular theology on their members. A way of living that is constantly questioning and revising itself in the company of equally committed and quizzical fellow travelers.

I began this retelling of Mark's testament as a personal meditation. If this happened today in my world, who would be the protagonists, what would it feel like, what would I make of the events and where would I stand vis a vis the person of Jesus? When I was younger I lived in an experimental religious community in Maltby, later I worked as a community development consultant all around Doncaster and its satellite towns. I have lived in Sheffield for a good part of my life though I studied and lived in East London for eight years. All this fed my imagination and Edlington, where I endeavoured set up a community forum, seemed an ideal place to situate a modern Christ. The Yorkshire Main Colliery, Edlington's pit, was deemed uneconomical and closed in 1985 and the town has expired slowly since then. This socio economic slump has been mirrored in towns all over South Yorkshire whether the main industry was coal, steel or train construction.

On a sabbatical in 2010 whilst tramping solo the Cumbria Way it dawned on me that the only way to capture the utterly surprising wisdom emanating from an uneducated, uncultured carpenter from the sticks was to make my Jesus figure a woman. In our society women are still not taken seriously and a largely male elite still resists the march of female emancipation. The one female prime minister we have had in the UK acted with such macho disregard for the consequences of her actions she might as well have been a man, as the village of Edlington with its poundshops and closed pubs and clubs silently testifies to thirty years later. To achieve the full shock value of Jesus social status it became obvious to me that a Hairdresser's daughter from a former pit village was a natural choice. How many people in our society today would expect to find a life-changing message in a person like Jess?

The most startling revelation I had whilst working on this project was that far from being difficult to imagine it was incredibly easy. As Mark Widdowson my fictitious journalist observes in his introduction 'what would make the powers that be in this country and beyond feel so threatened that they decided to do away with her?' Fundamentally challenge the system is the answer that will do it every time.

I also found that reality mimicked my imaginings. I came up with the idea of a mass cycle ride into London and the three days of action emanating from the steps of St Paul's a full year before the Occupy Movement staged a similar event in October 2011. I subsequently met a Traveller Lady on the streets of Doncaster who after giving me lucky heather told me I was writing a book and it would be successful! I also bumped into a man suffering Tourette's collecting for a charity to support his condition in a bookshop, he told me a very similar story to the one in blog eleven.

When I studied the New Testament we were told that Mark's gospel was the first to be transcribed (around 70AD) and that it was written in rather bald Koine (common) Greek. I decided that this would fit the style of a journalist and the form of a blog. Moving as fast as the events that it describes, posted from a laptop and lacking any of the descriptive subtleties of novelistic or academic prose, this hastily compiled testament would offer the subversive qualities of the first gospel.

Jess, like Jesus is a quiet revolutionary. She is a spark to fan to flame a growing movement for change and transformation. Jesus called this phenomenon the Kingdom of God, he did not call it the church. Jess calls it the Great Turning. This idea, like his, is not a religious term. His gave rise to metaphors from his everyday world: light, salt, scattered seed and great trees. The Great Turning was coined in a book of the same name by David C Korten and the notion of the Great Emergence by people like Joanna Macey and Phyllis Tickle. They sound the call asking us in the West to move from Empire to Earth Community, and for Jess that means the institutions that have seen themselves as the dispensers of Christianity have to face the fact that they have been seduced by the Imperial mind-set as much as any Bank or Multinational.

If those who read this feel that I have been unfaithful in some way to my source text and put too much of my own slant on the retelling then I suggest you try it for yourself. Write your own gospel based on your own setting - I suspect it will surprise you and hopefully leave you astonished, as I still am.

Adrian G R Scott
Christmas
2012

Further Reading

The Great Turning: From Empire to Earth Community by David C Korten
Berrett-Koehler (1 Nov 2007)

Coming Back to Life: Practices to Reconnect Our Lives, Our World by Joanna Macey and Molly Young Brown
New Society Publishers (11 Jan 1999)

The Great Emergence: How Christianity is Changing and Why: How Christianity Is Changing and Why by Phyllis Tickle
Baker Books, a division of Baker Publishing Group (1 Nov 2008)

Christology at the Crossroads by John Sobrino SJ
Orbis Books (USA) (15 Jun 1978)

Binding the Strong Man: A Political Reading of Mark's Story of Jesus by Ched Myers
Orbis Books; 20th Anniversary edition (24 Nov 2008)

The Message of Mark by Morna D Hooker
Epworth Press (2 April 1983)

Poor Man Called Jesus: Reflections on the Gospel of Mark by Jose Cardenas Pallares
Orbis Books (Dec 1990)

Jesus Before Christianity by Albert Nolan
Orbis Books (1 Sep 1990)

The Secret Message of Jesus: Uncovering the Truth That Could Change Everything Brian McLaren
Thomas Nelson (3 Feb 2012)

Everything Must Change: When the World's Biggest Problems and Jesus' Good News Collide by Brian McLaren
Thomas Nelson (1 Sep 2009)

The Gospel of Falling Down: The Beauty of Failure, in an Age of Success by Mark Townsend
O Books (26 Jan 2007)

We are Everywhere: The Irresistible Rise of Global Anti-capitalism by Notes from Nowhere
Verso Books; 1st Edition edition (3 Sep 2003)

The Shock Doctrine: The Rise of Disaster Capitalism Naomi Klein
Penguin; 1st edition (1 May 2008)

The Message Compact New Testament Paperback: New Testament, Psalms and Proverbs by Eugene H. Peterson
NavPress; First edition (15 Mar 2006)

Thanks to

Wilma Scott my wife for the artwork, both the Cover Portrait of Jess and the pencil drawing/collage of Mark Widdowson and for her constant encouragement and love.

Eva my eldest daughter for proof reading and giving me a perspective that is of the moment and to Lara my middle daughter and Tom my son for showing me what it means to deal with challenges in life. I love all three of you dearly.

To Jim Taylor of Seguin, Texas, USA for his strong encouragement to keep going with this project and his example of how to live the Jesus message. And to all who have offered hints and suggestions along the way.

David Loyn, Jess Hurd and Jason N Parkinson for a memorable afternoon at the Frontline Club in Paddington, I learnt more about journalism and journalists in that afternoon than any amount of research matter could teach.

To Marion Forrester for her kind proof reading and editing and showing me where a journey of real faith can take you. Peace and good to you.

All the scripture professors that schooled me painfully in Greek and taught me the art of interpretation.

All the groups I have introduced to the Jesus of the Gospels over the years.

The villages and people of South Yorkshire I have lived and worked in, of course Edlington and also Maltby, Rossington, Stainforth, Hexthorpe, Moorlands, and Highfields.

Finally to Mick Donelan the man who gave me the little brown plastic bound Good News New Testament and told me to read Mark's gospel and see where it might take me. It has taken me a long way Mick.

I took the photographs at the head of each Blog at the various places described. (Copyright 2012)